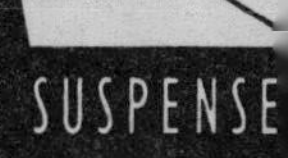

DOOMWATER

ROBERT LEESON

First published in Great Britain 1997
by Mammoth, an imprint of Reed International Books Ltd
Michelin House, 81 Fulham Road, London SW3 6RB
and Auckland, Melbourne, Singapore and Toronto

ISBN 0 7497 2765 9

10 9 8 7 6 5 4 3 2 1

A CIP catalogue record for this title is available from the British Library

Typeset by Avon Dataset Ltd, Bidford on Avon, Warwickshire
Printed in Great Britain by Cox & Wyman Ltd, Reading, Berkshire

Cover photograph from THE IMAGE BANK

Chapter One

Three drivers, front wheels on the white line, watched as the girl in the gaudily painted mini swept through the roundabout.

'Wouldn't mind a bit of that,' muttered the cowboy builder in the beat-up truck. He was so struck by what he saw that he forgot his golden rule – always cut across a roundabout in front of a woman driver.

From his high seat in the tanker cab, the middle-aged man smiled to himself at the lurid colours of the little car and at the vivid red of its owner's hair and thought of his own daughter. The girl in the mini must be seventeen, he guessed, and he wondered how *she* got on with her parents.

Through the broad windscreen of the silver limo, the chauffeur's trained eye took in the speeding car and, at the same time, exchanged glances with his passenger through the driving mirror. There was a slight, answering nod.

Three engines revved, three vehicles moved

forward into and through the roundabout. But the mini and the redhead had vanished from the road before them.

As she guided her car along the side streets into the residential area of town, Charlotte Dawson was totally unaware that she had caught the eye of these men, unknown to her.

She was used to attention, of course. With her mother's slim figure and blue eyes, her father's fiery hair and wayward temper, she knew people stared at her – often for the wrong reasons. But she had no vanity at all.

She stood out in a crowd and not for her looks and personality alone. She was the star of the art department at her college. Her teachers foresaw a great future for her.

At the-end-of year exhibition, her landscape picture had dominated the show, with its passion and force, its atmosphere of foreboding. Any visitor entering the hall found their eyes drawn to it. And one visitor did more than look.

Though he would not give his name, he had bought the picture on the spot and paid such a price that

Charlotte, only weeks after passing her driving test, had been able to buy her first car – second-hand, but a mover. Like its owner.

She was going places. She was a golden girl. Only the shrewdest eye, though, could see beyond the good looks, the talent, the quick success, to something else.

Her picture sent a different message. Looking down from an old bridge with a broken rail, through a veil of looming trees, deep, dark water stretched away, magnetic, menacing. Somewhere in the middle a pale arm was lifted above the surface, a last desperate signal, before the unknown victim was drawn down into the infinity of death.

Studying this picture, the viewers, even her tutors, wondered how lively, gifted, handsome Charlotte Dawson could paint such an awesome, gloom-laden work. And call it 'Doomwater.'

The answer was simple, but terrible.

Often, Charlotte Dawson wished that she were dead – no, not dead – just vanished under the waters that flowed through her waking thoughts and sleeping nightmares.

Chapter Two

Charlotte pulled up in a quiet, tree-lined avenue, in front of a tall, old house, scooped her art things from the back seat and walked along the weed-covered path, then up several stone steps. The front door, paint peeling slightly, squealed as she opened it.

Inside there was a faint, old smell, of books and papers. Her feet struck a hollow note on the stairs. She called out, 'It's me.' There was no answer and she did not really expect one.

Gran wasn't home. If you wanted to catch her in you needed an appointment. She was out at a meeting – a good cause, a campaign, whatever. She might not be home till midnight. Or she might suddenly appear, like a disorganised genie, shouting from the basement, 'Charlie, come and eat!'

Charlotte was used to all this. She had grown accustomed to it since she was twelve and came to this old house not just to visit, but to stay for good.

At the top of the third flight of stairs she came to

a door half-covered by a huge art poster. She knocked up the latch with her elbow and went in, kicking the door shut behind her.

Inside, the high-ceilinged room was bathed in light from the late-afternoon sun. It had windows on three sides. Gran had let her move into it as combined flat and studio. She never came in, unless invited, and left Charlotte to run it exactly as she liked. The result was that the curtained-off living area, on the blank wall, was neat and tidy, a total contrast to the chaos of the art side with its half-worked canvasses stacked up, an old packing case littered with still-life objects.

And fixed on an easel, half-finished, was a portrait of a shy, rather ugly young man, with large glasses halfway down his nose.

Charlotte went over to the cluttered sink, filled a kettle with water, made coffee and then sat in front of one window. The sun, now going down, cast long shadows over the houses – and into her mind.

She thought once more, as she had been thinking all the way home from college, of the next day. It was the start of the holidays, weeks of freedom from timetables, getting up early, working to order, taking account of other people, crowds, push, shove, chatter, excitement, gossip, laughter, malice . . .

But the thought brought her no pleasure. Instead her mind roamed forwards and backwards on a dire and unremitting pendulum, each swing carrying her further down into helplessness and despair.

Tomorrow she would travel twenty miles to a country churchyard, where in the shade of a thousand-year-old yew tree, she would lay flowers before a headstone with a stark and simple inscription:

Roger Dawson
born 28th July 1954, died 28th July 1990
Frances Dawson
born 19th May 1955, died 28th July 1990

Each month Charlotte made this pilgrimage, without fail, in sunshine or rain, summer or winter. Tomorrow would be the sixtieth time. One half of her shrank from the journey, the other half knew that she had to go.

She must go and stand by her parents' grave while the question hammered at her brain: Why have they gone and why am I still here?

As the pendulum reached its extreme point and

began its return curve, back through time, so her thoughts dived with dizzying speed, across five years to the sea, mountains, sun, fire and death.

Chapter Three

She was twelve again, thin, excitable, moody, a constant spark to her father's explosive nature, with her mother smiling and calm, separating them, calming them, teasing them.

A last-minute holiday on Santa Vittoria, on doctor's orders. Her father's money-making drive had taken its toll of his health. They booked a villa in a small group on a hill over a beautiful bay.

There were other families, other children – games, tricks, fights, swimming, sunbathing. Charlotte would watch while the others threw themselves into the blue waves, splashing, leaping, shouting for her to join them.

But she would not swim. She could not keep away from water. It drew her, pulled her, but she dared not go in. For she knew with a certainty that matched her fascination, that once she entered the water, it would close over her. She would drift down, powerless in its green, dark depths, while others laughed and yelled unheeding in the sunlight above.

And now her fearful daydream focused like a film close-up.

The villa bedroom. Her father and mother dressed to go out, she still in T-shirt and jeans. His face reddening, eyes gleaming with fury, her own face pale with rage. Her mother, for once silent, watching, amazed at their passion.

They had planned a birthday supper for him at a famous restaurant in the hills. He had decided to drive by the inland route. Charlotte had demanded they go by the sea. How could he understand her longing to see the red sun swallowed up in the blue-green waters, from the safety of the coastal road?

He had shouted at her, 'This stupid obsession of yours with water – it has to stop now. You'll come with us by the hill route. Get changed.'

She had screamed back, 'I won't, I won't!' She had stormed back into her own room, her anger suddenly gripping her behind the eyes like a vice. She lay down on the bed, her head full of a sickening, dark pain. Her mother came in, stroking, soothing, but she only turned her back.

At last she was left alone. After an interval –

minutes, hours? – she heard her father call from below the bedroom window, 'Charlotte, are you coming? We won't wait for ever.'

Those were his last words to her. Car doors slammed, the engine roared and her parents drove out of her life. Half an hour later, somewhere on a bend high in the hills, the car left the road, crashed through a barrier, somersaulted down the ravine wall, burst into flames and was consumed.

When the news was brought to the villa by the police, later that evening, a curtain came down on Charlotte's mind, cutting off the past, leaving only one image, five words. Five years later, in the bleak depths of her mood, Charlotte still heard them clearly, ringing through her head, 'We won't wait for ever.'

She *knew* it was not a guess, she was convinced that if she had not quarrelled with her father, inflaming his quick, rash anger, this would not have happened. If only, if only she had gone with them, then they might still all three be alive together. Or, if not that, then she would have gone with them, for ever.

Now all she could do was long for the deep waters of her mind to take her in and still her nightmare.

Chapter Four

Charlotte's eyes turned to the desk in the corner of her studio space. Strewn with books and scraps of paper, it was as chaotic as the rest of the sunlit room.

But she knew exactly what was there and her mind fixed on one sheet of paper which lay in the centre of the desk top, together with the envelope it came in. She knew its message by heart now.

Earlier in the term an invitation had come in the post to write off for a free horoscope, one to cover an entire month ahead. From the time she was twelve until she started college and work had begun to fill her time more and more, Charlotte had spent pocket money on astrological magazines. She had read predictions not in a dreamy, wish-fulfilment way, but with a purpose, as if in some way she could discover what she might do with a life that in her darkest moments would seem aimless, pointless.

Someone must have got hold of her address from those days and written with the horoscope offer, adding a condition which intrigued her and made her reply. The horoscope would be free provided she would take part in a test, which, said the letter, would help demonstrate that astrology really worked.

During the month of the horoscope she must record what happened to her, the main, significant events, not trivial everyday things. This 'diary' would be compared week by week with what had been forecast. But the facts must be set down coolly, as they unfolded, no attempt must be made to fit them to the predictions, as enthusiasts did, or make nonsense of them, as sceptics tried to do.

In the end Charlotte had sent off her reply, with details of her birth, but in the bustle and excitement of the end-of-year exhibition being set up, she forgot about it. Last week the horoscope had arrived. She had read it, once, twice, three times until she could remember each word.

PISCES

When you were born, Sun, Moon, Mercury and Venus crowded into your sign. Inevitably all your virtues and defects have been intensified. Imaginative, quick-

witted, yet easily confused, clear-sighted in creative things, chaotic and disorganised in the every day; outgoing, sympathetic, keenly aware of others, yet easily manipulated by those who seek to use you. Like the water which is the essence of your sign, the sea of your ruling planet Neptune, you have hidden depths and currents in your nature which fascinate and alarm you. For you only art – or love – can bring this turbulence under control. For them, you will risk anything.

It seemed to have been written by someone who had known her all her life, had lived with her and watched her closely. Then came the predictions:

At first the Sun in Leo brings self-expression and creativity together. You will have success in your chosen work and it will be no flash in the pan. For Mercury and Venus are in the same sign and love offers the same promise as art. A chance encounter will intrigue and excite.

A great rush of self-confidence will carry you on, ignoring friendly warnings which, rather than steadying you, will only provoke you. You know where you are going and will listen to no one but the voice inside you.

But, in the third week, these heavenly bodies and the Moon will move into Virgo, your opposing sign. All will now be risk and confusion.

Who can you trust? Who is telling you the truth? As a new, exciting relationship develops, must an old, tried and trusted one be shattered?

At this point, Mars leaves the harmony of Libra to enter the intensity of Scorpio, a sign of water like your own, and one of a significance as yet unknown to you.

As this chosen period draws to its climax Pluto, whose message is elimination, enters Scorpio. Some resolution of all your problems is drawing near, but is it to be an end to ambitions or to anxieties? It will be at your choice.

All will be resolved in the flood of events – one way or another.

Charlotte's mind ran over these words. The first week of the month had passed. Should she sit down and write her verdict on what had happened? It was clear enough to her that 'success in your chosen work' could not be more true.

Next came the promise of love. Against her reason and good sense, the thought excited her. But beyond that all was uncertainty, risk, even threat, menace. Did she want to go through all that?

Then she laughed at herself. Whether she believed or not, whether she wrote down what happened to her or not, it would still happen. She wasn't a kid any more to imagine that if she shut her eyes and didn't look, it wouldn't be there.

And inside her something deeper urged her on, to go into the future, promise or threat, to take it, not just let it overwhelm her, to put an end to the uncertainties and guilts that haunted her, to find it, not to let it find her.

With these thoughts an unbearable tension seized her.

As she was sitting there, the studio had grown darker; furniture, easels, pictures took on strange shapes in the dim light. She reached urgently for her pen, and switched on the desk lamp. In an instant the darkness around her grew more intense.

In that moment she heard behind her the creaking of the door. She turned, heart leaping inside her.

In the gap formed by the opening door, a last ray of the sun caught a strange shape which was reaching into the room, a face grotesque and greenish, lips gross and trembling, eyes protruding.

Charlotte screamed.

Chapter Five

In a flash, Charlotte's fear was overtaken by anger. Leaping up she flew at the intruder, grappling and snatching with her hands for a hold. Her scrabbling fingers caught on the loathsome face.

To her horror it began to disintegrate in her grasp and come away from the head.

A voice cut across her nightmare, plaintive and edged with hysterical laughter.

'Knock it off, Charlie. You're pulling my hair out by the roots.'

Charlotte let the intruder go and snapped on the light switch by the door.

'Ker, you idiot!' She collapsed in giggles and for a second or two leant against the small figure in the doorway. Then she threw aside the remains of the tattered mask still clinging to her fingers and, shaking her head, looked sternly at the young man who stood there blinking in the bright studio lights. A sudden thought struck her.

'How did you get in? Gran's not home.'

'Right! But some stupid and totally irresponsible person, probably an artist with an inflated ego, left the front door open.'

Charlotte's hand flew to her mouth. She reached wildly for her handbag. Ker shook his head pityingly, then held out his hand.

'Here, you left the keys in the lock as well.' He went on, mockingly, 'This week, carelessness will bring near-tragedy. Only the quick-thinking and thoughtfulness of a reliable and long-suffering friend will see you through.'

'Oh, shut up!' she retorted. But there was something in what Ker said, she knew. He was a long-suffering and reliable friend – real name Matthew Harris. They had teamed up in the junior school. He with his sharp awareness rescuing her belongings where her forgetfulness had scattered them. She with her warm impulsiveness defending him when other kids jeered at his looks and size. They made an odd couple, she four inches taller than Ker and as good-looking as he was not.

At school, it hadn't been long before he was called Kermit, shortened to Ker, and behind their backs,

Charlotte and he were known as the Princess and the Frog.

They had remained inseparable right into college where Ker was in Media Studies. If Charlotte wanted to explain to herself why their friendship had lasted all of ten years, she could only say, 'We have fantastic arguments but never quarrel.'

But they were just good friends, stupid as that sounded. Charlotte didn't give a damn about looks, but you can't have a lover four inches shorter than yourself, can you?

One of her girl friends said slyly, 'Why not kiss Ker, for real? He might turn into a prince,' and Charlotte had quipped back, 'Or I might turn into a frog.'

There was another motive. Charlotte knew that Ker's friendship was a fixed point in her life and she did not want to lose its easy, bantering warmth by trying to change their relationship.

Ker slumped down on to a chair. 'Coffee,' he moaned. 'I must have coffee. I did a good deed and I got abused and assaulted.'

'Aaaah,' she jeered, but she went and filled the kettle all the same and put it on the small gas ring by the sink.

Handing him the coffee mug she demanded, 'Why this monster mask? You almost scared me out of my wits.'

Ker eyed her, weighing his words. 'I thought you might like to do some more work on that portrait,' he nodded to the easel. 'I was going to match my appearance to your drawing.' He chuckled, 'When I found the front door open, I couldn't resist putting the mask on and sneaking upstairs.'

'Idiot! Anyway,' Charlotte nodded to the picture, 'that's you to the life. I haven't altered anything. Artists always stick to the truth, at all costs.'

'Yeah,' he said, 'and journalists always stick to the facts.'

Both laughed and sat down, coffee in hand. Charlotte shrugged, 'Anyway, it's too late for another session now. The light's gone. And to be honest, I'm not in the mood.'

He looked at her more closely, part sympathetic, part reproving. 'Brooding again, Charlie?' Then he spoke more briskly, nodding to her desk. 'Horoscopes again? That rubbish won't make matters any easier. No scientific basis for it at all.'

'Huh,' she said. 'No basis? How do you explain

that I, a Pisces, have gone in for art and you, a Gemini, are going in for journalism?'

She should have kept quiet. Ker's eyes gleamed. 'I've been reading this book . . .' That was his favourite opening gambit.

Charlotte laughed. 'Surprise me.'

'In this book they reckon that artists are more likely to be Cancer and so are businessmen and engineers. Pisceans are musicians.'

'Same difference,' she retorted. But he went on, 'And Geminis are more likely to be lawyers, advertising people or clergymen.'

'All word spinners, aren't they,' Charlotte shot back.

Ker laughed, 'OK, OK, there you are. If it fits, believe it. Anyway,' he went on with a broad smile, 'not so much of your "going in for journalism". From Monday on, I am a journalist.'

'Oh, Ker.' She leaned over and hugged him. 'Congratulations.'

He shrugged. 'Well, the truth is I've got a holiday job, six weeks with the *Evening Sentinel*, in their library.'

'Books again.'

'Nah. Records. Database. You name it. The reporters on assignments come to me and say, "What's the word about so-and-so?" '

'And you dig the dirt?'

'I,' replied Ker, with dignity, 'find out all the relevant material, background, biographical stuff. Sounds boring. Not quite what I'm after. But, it's a start.'

Then his voice changed. 'Listen, Charlie, I meant to tell you. When I came up the road just now, there was a bloke who seemed to be nosing around your car. But the light wasn't all that good and anyway he cleared off when I got near. Dressed in a dark suit, almost uniform.'

She chuckled, 'Off-duty traffic warden, practising. Art dealer going to make me an offer for my trim. All sorts of things.'

Ker made a face. 'Don't you take anything seriously?' He paused. 'Of course, you do, one thing . . .'

His voice trailed off as though he'd said too much. But she knew what he meant and suddenly she thought again of the next day and her journey to the church and her parents' grave.

'Ker,' she began, then stopped. From the basement came the sudden clatter of pans and crockery.

Then Gran's voice, trained to top pitch in many a meeting and demonstration, echoed through the house, 'Char—lie! Will you ask that idiot who left his bike lying across the garden path and nearly broke my ankle, if he's staying for supper?'

Chapter Six

Five miles from the churchyard where her parents were buried, Charlotte's car came to a halt, without warning. Luckily she was in a broad country road and driving near the grass verge. No one was trying to pass her. That was the trouble: there was no sign of help, either.

How could she have broken down? The dealer had sworn, cross his heart, that the engine was as sound as a bell. Would you buy a second-hand car from a man like that?

Charlotte tried the ignition again. At the turn of the key the engine spluttered and died. What to do? Should she get out and look at the engine? What good would that do? She didn't know a carburettor from a camshaft.

A moment's exasperation came and went. She made up her mind and got out of the car. The only thing to do was to walk to Little Morley and look for a helpful garage hand. The day was fine, the sky clear and blue and the sun was not yet at its full height. A walk would calm her down.

Reaching into the back seat she carefully lifted out the flowers she had bought, in their plastic wrapping. She was standing with them in her arms when someone spoke, a confident, cultivated voice, with an echo of some regional accent, maybe Midlands.

'Can I help? You don't want to be late for your date, do you?'

Charlotte jumped. The silver-grey limo had whispered to a stop beside her, the back window silently lowered and a dark, bearded young man was smiling easily at her. In front the uniformed chauffeur looked straight ahead.

'It's not a date,' said Charlotte, confused. She felt her cheeks were warm. Was she turning red? 'I'm going to the church at Little Morley. My parents are buried there. The car just stopped.'

Her voice died. Why was she telling a complete stranger all this?

He seemed to read her thoughts. The easy, even flirtatious smile vanished from his face, the door opened and he stood there, stylish in shirt and slacks which must have set him back more than the little car which had just given up the ghost, cost her.

'May I?' But he was already opening her car door. He shook his head, tut-tutted. 'Aha, nothing serious. Just forgot to fill the tank, didn't we?'

'I didn't!' Charlotte was indignant and now she was sure she was blushing. Because she realised she could not remember when she last bought petrol. She calmed herself and forced a laugh.

'Silly me! Thanks, anyway. That's a big relief. I can pick some up in Little Morley, when I've been to the church.'

His eyebrows rose. 'It's all of five miles.'

'So? A walk will do me good.'

He laughed openly, showing perfect white teeth. Now she looked at him directly and noticed that though his face was tanned, under the darkness of the beard she could see the faint white lines of a scar on his chin.

'I have a better idea, I think. I'll give you a lift to Little Morley. While you are in the church, Arnold,' the chauffeur gave a slight nod, 'will pick up some petrol for you and then we'll drive you back.'

'You're very kind, but I couldn't,' Charlotte protested. 'You must have . . .'

He interrupted her, still smiling. 'I do have things I must attend to. But since I'm my own master, I shall give myself an hour off to do a good deed.

'Please,' he added, almost pleadingly.

His voice had lightened and she realised for the first time that he was not so much older than her. The opulence of the limo, the chauffeur, the clothes, had misled her. He was nineteen, twenty, no more. This decided her.

'Thank you. I will.'

He opened the limo door and stood back. Then as she sank into the deep soft leather of the rear seat he followed her, holding out her keys.

'I locked the door. OK?' He signalled and the car moved away down the road. Charlotte looked out of the window, furious with herself, then had to laugh.

'You must think I'm an idiot. Forgetting the petrol. Forgetting to lock the car door.'

'Not at all. I'm a businessman. If I forget things I hire people to remember them for me. Besides,' he looked sideways at her, 'an artist is entitled to be absent-minded. It goes with the work, doesn't it?'

Her mouth opened. 'How do you know I'm an artist?'

'I'm afraid I looked at the equipment on the back seat. Guessing is part of my work.'

'And what is that?' she asked boldly.

'Some people wouldn't call it work. They'd call it gambling. Playing with money. It's wearying, mind you, nerve-wracking now and then, but with all the excitement of a game.'

Charlotte looked away. She did not care for speculators. She knew Ker despised them. But this man was so young, so open.

Yet, brokers, traders, dealers, they were all young these days, weren't they? Jumping up and down, waving shirt-sleeved arms in front of their computer screens. But the images from television, the open mouths, flushed faces, wild shouts and signals, this man didn't fit that at all. He looked more like a third-year student, even a junior lecturer at college.

While she puzzled he spoke, 'My name's Conrad. Conrad Durrant. And I'm an orphan, too.'

Chapter Seven

Suspicion, even anger, suddenly swept into Charlotte's mind. She answered sharply.

'You seem to know a lot about me, Mr Durrant.'

The light died in his eyes. He spoke apologetically. 'I am sorry. My habit of guessing. But you did say your parents were buried at Little Morley.'

Embarrassment and relief came as swiftly as the anger. Impulsively she laid a hand on his arm. The shirt fabric was smooth and cool.

'No. I should say sorry. I'd forgotten I told you about the church. My name's Charlotte – Dawson. And I'm sorry that you're an . . .'

He shrugged. 'Don't be. I never really knew my . . . parents. I've had to live without them for ever. Not like you, I guess, having them and losing them.'

She nodded and, with a quick, almost shy look, he went on, 'Will you call me Conrad?'

She answered warmly, as if to put matters right. 'OK, and, it's Charlotte.'

'Thank you. You know, I feel this is somehow more than just a chance encounter,' he said, and now once more suspicion whispered in Charlotte's mind. 'Or a pick-up,' he added swiftly, 'though you've good reason to be wary. I mean, I didn't actually say "we've met before somewhere", but it was very close to that.'

She smiled. 'Strangely enough, I did have the feeling I'd met you before.'

Now he looked wary. 'Some people say I'm a bit like that actor on . . . I can never remember the series anyway, I never watch television. Computer screens are my viewing.'

Charlotte grinned at that. Self-mockery from a speculator. That was a good sign. Something made her go on, 'I wonder whether any meeting is by chance,' she began and was on the edge of mentioning the horoscope when he said quickly, dismissively almost, 'Oh, I'm not into destinies. I only go for what I can calculate, futures.' He smiled at his own word-play then, as if to change the subject, he glanced out of the car window and said, 'Hello, here's Little Morley coming up now. My favourite village. It's a lovely little place. I'd be happy if they put me in this churchyard.'

'Oh.' His remark shocked Charlotte. She tried to laugh it off. 'That's a long time ahead.'

He laughed too. 'Time passes quickly. Look how soon those five miles went.'

Turning, he said, 'Charlotte. We'll wait by the gate, here. You take your time.'

'Are you sure?'

'Sure I'm sure. We'll wait.'

The light mood which had blown into her mind during the brief car ride slowly ebbed as Charlotte walked along the gravel path of the churchyard, flowers over her arm. Her feet, knowing the way as well as her eyes did, turned from the path on to the short green turf, among old grey headstones, marble angel statues and the simple plastic urns with their wilting flower stems.

At each step the tide of depression flowed higher. The English summer day, the smell of cut grass, began to fade and a hotter sun, a browner landscape, filled her mind. Second by second she was back year by year, to that villa bedroom – her father's angry face, her mother's troubled eyes.

Her feet struck the edge of a grave. There was the white headstone:

Roger Dawson . . . Frances Dawson.

The plain inscription accused her more than any statement of her guilt. Blindly she knelt, lifting out the dead flowers. Then swiftly she moved to the wall near the church, bent over the tap and filled the vase again, returned to the grave and began to thrust in new stems, ruffling, arranging the heads, mechanically darting out a hand to pick out a weed she had spotted in the short grass.

At last Charlotte could kneel in front of their names no longer. Dropping the rest of the flowers she rose, turned, stumbled, then ran, tripping on stone edges and grass clumps, to the path, and still she ran.

The air around her was suddenly cold and dark. Her feet sounded hollow beneath her. They had carried her into the church. Pews, aisle, stretched away in front of her in the half-light, the smell of old stone and emptiness filling her nostrils.

She tried to turn and run out through the open church door but her legs gave way and she sank to her knees, facing the stone wall deep in shadow, dark, forbidding, blocking her way. Stay there, it said, stay there and face the truth.

She tried to rise and could not, tried to close her eyes, but they would not. Her gaze was fixed upon the wall which was blank no longer.

As if a film were projected on the stone surface she saw her father and mother as clearly as if they stood within her reach, but now they were walking away and leaving her.

Violent sickening pain gripped her head so that she almost fainted. Clearly, as five years before on this very day, she heard her father's voice: 'We won't wait for ever.'

The voices in her head were suddenly pierced by a wailing cry. It came from deep inside her as the tears flooded down her face.

Chapter Eight

Someone's arm was round her shoulder, a hand beneath her elbow, raising her up and, very gently, leading her out into the sunlight. Without raising her head she knew who it was.

'Charlotte.' He spoke almost in a whisper. 'Here.' He pressed a large white handkerchief into her hand, then let go of her arm and stood a little way away from her.

The simple act of wiping her eyes, dabbing her face, brought a measure of relief to her tormented mind. Shame, embarrassment that he should have been there in the church and seen her outburst, brought her back into the present and into reality. The sunlight, too, was real, not blinding and hot, but gently warm.

'What you need is a drink and a meal.' Conrad had taken her arm again and was leading her down the gravel walk.

'I don't . . .' she stammered, but he led her on

firmly, saying, 'Don't worry about the flowers. I fixed them.'

'You . . . ?'

'Yes. I'm sorry if it seems pushy but I felt like walking through the graveyard. I saw the flowers lying there. So, guessing again, I felt something wasn't right, and I followed you into the church.'

Conrad walked her steadily on, chatting about all kinds of things. Charlotte neither remembered what he said nor what she replied, until she found herself in an armchair by a window, overlooking a hotel garden.

'Drink this. Just a little brandy.'

It burnt her throat. She coughed and suddenly felt normal again.

'You must think I'm crazy. I'm not really the hysterical type you know.'

Conrad shook his head. 'I wish I could feel like that about my parents, but I just feel nothing. It's empty in here.' He tapped his chest.

'You don't know how lucky you are,' Charlotte began, then said, 'no, that's selfish. I have to live with my feelings, you with yours.'

'You mean, it's in the stars?' he asked more lightly.

Once again the impulse came to tell him of her horoscope. Today's meeting fitted so truly into its pattern, it was uncanny. But some uncertainty kept her from speaking. Instead, she spoke as lightly as he had done.

'Let's change the subject. Tell me more about your work.'

For a moment they were interrupted by a waiter arriving with sandwiches. Conrad made a face at her. 'No, not more about my work, please. It is truly boring unless you are into it, like those card games people go nuts about and you can't even understand the rules.'

While she laughed, he went on, 'Now what you do is much more interesting, in anybody's language. Tell me about that. Go on. You do owe me a little, eh?'

So she told him of her work at college, the exhibition, her picture, the secret, surprise buyer.

'What was this picture like? It must have made an impression on someone.'

She described 'Doomwater'. He listened closely, nodding as she talked.

'You put all you had, all your secret thoughts and

fears, into that, didn't you?' His eyes gleamed with an intensity that took her aback.

She answered evasively, 'I suppose so. There's always more in a painting than even the artist knows.'

As they finished their meal, he said, 'You know, I live at Harford Mill.'

'Oh, that's near where I live.'

He grinned, like a boy. 'Oh, really? I only took over the place last month. We're still installing the hardware. Not much left of the original Old Mill, but there's a fine house and park.'

'Right.' Charlotte spoke eagerly. 'Lots of people would like to paint there. The owners used to allow people in, but recently the message has been "Private, keep out".'

'Not any more – at least to you,' answered Conrad. He drew out a slim wallet and, selecting a card, passed it to her, having signed it on the back.

'Come when you like, to paint. You can have the run of the grounds. Just show the card at the gatehouse.' He paused and eyed her warily. 'If you're . . . doubtful . . . bring a friend. Stop for tea. I may even be home.'

'Thanks,' Charlotte breathed. She couldn't think

of anything more to say, though her thoughts were racing – excited, confused.

He rose, 'Come on, Charlotte. I'll take you back to your car. You've had enough of Durrant for one day. Arnold's got your petrol by now.'

She reached for her shoulder bag, but he shook his head, laughing, 'Don't pay me for it, pay him. He carries the cash. I never have any. Come on.'

Later that afternoon Charlotte sat in her studio. She was drawing Conrad's face from memory, sketching in the high forehead, deep-set brown eyes, dark beard.

And, underneath the beard, that scar whose silvery lines intrigued her strangely.

Some stray wisp of memory like smoke blew across her mind. Had she met or seen Conrad Durrant before? Then it was gone.

Before she realised it, she had put Conrad's sketch on the easel alongside Ker's half-finished portrait. The contrast made her uneasy – the suave handsome and the eager ugly.

Shaking her head to dispel the thought she took up Conrad's likeness and skimmed it across the room. It fell on the desk, lying next to the horoscope paper.

A chance encounter will intrigue and excite. She stared at the words, then laughed at herself and put the kettle on.

Chapter Nine

Charlotte's days passed slowly now. It was always the same when holidays started, impossible to get going with anything.

But now, far from enjoying her idleness, she grew more restless by the day. She worked a while on the sketch she had made of Conrad, then put it aside in frustration and worked on Ker's portrait. But she got nowhere with that, either.

Ker himself was busy with his job at the *Evening Sentinel.* He had vanished from view for the moment. Other college friends were away with their families.

Charlotte wandered down into town and back again, then got into her car (remembering to check the tank) and drove through the country lanes. Before she knew it she was driving past Harford Mill.

The estate's high walls were hung over with creepers. A small red-brick lodge stood guard over a massive iron gate. The house itself was invisible behind a screen of trees. She stopped the car and looked but did not go in. Something, maybe shyness, held her back.

Or maybe it was just caution. People who throw out invitations may not be over the moon if you take them at their word.

Part of her wanted very much to see Harford Mill – and its new owner. Part of her held back. What would happen if they met again? Was there a hidden meaning in that chance meeting, which dovetailed so completely with the horoscope?

If things were set to work out, then they would. Nothing Charlotte could do could alter the pattern of events. Inside her, though, she did not quite believe that. She felt an urge to make things happen. And yet she did nothing. Day followed day and the restlessness grew until it was almost painful.

In the end, it was Ker who made things happen. Late one afternoon she came back from roving around town to find her studio door open. Inside, Ker sat by her desk, reading.

As she entered he leapt up and said, 'Hi!' in a too loud voice, then added quickly, 'Gran said I could come up and wait for you.'

Charlotte smiled to herself. Ker said 'Gran' not

'your gran', as though he were one of the family. Then she thought wryly, why not? There wasn't much of a family, room for one more, like a brother.

They chatted as she made coffee, both a little awkward. Ker obviously had something on his mind and at last he burst out, 'I couldn't help reading this.' He held up the horoscope sheet. 'You're not seriously going to write down everything that happens to you and send it off to a complete stranger?'

'Why not?' she answered. 'It's a sort of research project, testing whether horoscopes work or not. It's scientific. You ought to approve.'

He put down his cup and walked to and fro. 'But you don't know who they are. Giving them all these personal details. It's an invasion of privacy.'

She laughed, 'Come on, Ker.' She pointed to her half-completed diary, 'There's nothing confidential there. A reporter from the *Sentinel* would want far more than that.'

Ker made a face, but said nothing. Her eyes were racing over the written paper. Her heart missed a beat then returned to normal. The account of the trip to Little Morley had missed out the scene in the church. Some instinct had made her censor that.

Maybe fear of thinking about it. She shivered. Then she noticed that Ker was looking at her, puzzled by her expression. She forced a quick laugh, 'You have to admit, Ker, what's happened to me does fit the prediction.'

'Huh! You can make any events fit any prediction. People make fortunes out of it every day of the week. It all hangs on how you interpret them.'

'OK.' She was stung by his derisive tone. 'You interpret them for me.'

He did not answer for a while but walked to the window and looked out, then he swung round, his face serious.

'All right. How's this for a pattern? This encounter on the way to the church wasn't chance or accidental. Supposing it were a set-up. Not fate, destiny, but manipulation.'

'Set-up?' Her voice was half-mocking, half-angry.

'Yes, suppose your petrol tank had been tapped so that you ran out on the road. You remember I saw this bloke near your car – now, don't interrupt, Charlie – let me finish. Just as you break down, this bloke arrives. Amazing timing, amazingly helpful. He spends half his day driving you to the church, gives you lunch. And he's supposed to be somebody whose time *is* money.'

Charlotte hesitated. 'Well . . . if it was a pick-up he didn't come on very strong. He was just interested in my work. He invited me to go and paint at Harford Mill. Look!'

She held out Conrad Durrant's card. Ker turned it over. 'Admit any time,' he read. He looked keenly at Charlotte. 'Do you really trust this bloke?'

'Well, I certainly don't believe he fixed my car so he could pick me up in a country lane.'

'Hey, Charlie,' Ker became serious again. 'You've no idea who bought your picture, have you? Suppose it was this Durrant bloke. This could get creepy.'

Now Charlotte protested, 'Oh, Ker. You call yourself a sceptic, but you'll believe anything. I don't think investigative journalism's doing you any good. You used to be such a nice person.'

'Nice people have to watch their backs, Charlie!'

'Hey, this bloke has got under your skin and you haven't even met him.'

'As long as he doesn't get under yours!'

The two of them stared at one another. Charlotte said, 'This is getting heavy, Ker. Look, I want to go and paint at Harford Mill. It's a fantastic spot. He's invited me to do just that. The fact is, I've been hesitating.'

'Sign of good sense at last.'

'Knock it off, Ker. Listen, Conrad said, "bring a friend". Right. You're my friend, aren't you? You come with me. I get to paint, you get to investigate his set-up. If it is dodgy you win. Either way we both get to do what we want.'

Ker put his head on one side. 'Hey, Pisceans are supposed to be manipulative, aren't they?' Then he grinned. 'You're on, mate.'

Chapter Ten

As the car took the bend in the Harford Mill estate road and the house came into view, Charlotte gasped in surprise and pleasure.

It stood on rising ground. A broad front of mellow golden stone, with white pillars on either side of the main doors, shone in the morning sun. Around the house and beyond into the distance stretched green parkland and woods. From the right where the ground fell away, came the gleam of water and the faint roar of a weir.

'It's fantastic.'

Ker nodded, impressed, 'Must have cost him a whole day's trading profits.'

'You are so cynical. You're eaten up with envy,' she mocked.

'Uh, huh,' he shook his head. 'Not my scene. Couldn't stand wearing red braces and making silly signs all day. Anyway, tomorrow he could be flat broke – or in jail.'

‘I don’t think Conrad Durrant is easy come, easy go,’ said Charlotte. ‘Anyway,’ she added as the car pulled up in front of the pillars. ‘Judge for yourself. There he is.’

Conrad stood on the steps, hands linked, feet slightly apart, in a dark suit. He looked impressive, Charlotte thought. Hard to remember he was – oh – two years older than her and no more.

Conrad shook hands, giving them both the same, slightly shy smile, then led the way in through the hall, waving a hand to left and to right, ‘It all happens down here. Upstairs is sleeping and formal eating. When there’s time.’

Ker looked around, curious. Through open doors he could see desks, computers, heard a subdued hum and clatter.

A young woman appeared, shrewd eyes beneath tightly-curled dark hair, slim in a dark suit covered by a loose, half-open white overall.

‘Angela,’ Conrad spoke easily. ‘Meet Charlotte and . . .’ Ker blushed and muttered, ‘Matthew Harris.’

‘Matthew,’ repeated Angela with a smile. Conrad went on, ‘Angela is really in charge here.’

Angela gave Charlotte a quick up and down

glance, then turned to smile again at Ker, as if anticipating Conrad's next words, 'Angie, love, can you take over? I have to go into town.'

To Charlotte he said, 'Sorry, the story of my life. Angela will point you to the Old Mill and, if Matthew's interested, she'll show him how we operate here, which she knows better than I do.

'I'll be back about one and if you can bear to wait perhaps we can all have a spot of lunch. Must go now. 'Bye – have a good day.'

The morning passed quickly. Charlotte roamed the estate, stopping to admire and to sketch, while back at the house Ker chatted and argued with the quick-witted, formidable Angela.

They met again over lunch, served in a small dining-room whose broad windows looked out over the park. But Conrad was not there. A phone message told them he was held up – but come again – both!

As they drove away, Ker spoke quietly. 'If only half of what I heard is true, Conrad Durrant must be very seriously rich. And only nineteen too, so Angela says.'

'And why shouldn't it be true?'

'Because this whole money-makes-money game is virtual reality, that's why. I'm not saying anybody's lying. It's just not real. But I'd like to know more. How he got his start. Were his parents loaded, or what?'

'He never knew them.' Charlotte spoke so sharply that Ker looked at her in surprise.

'Oh, I see.' He paused, then said, 'Sorry for rabbitting on. Did you have a good day?'

'Oh, yes,' Charlotte answered absent-mindedly. 'Saw a lot of things I'd like to paint.'

She did not go on and Ker asked no more questions. They each returned to their own thoughts.

And Charlotte's thoughts were in turmoil. She could not tell Ker what was on her mind.

That morning as she roamed the estate with her sketchpad she had come upon the Old Mill, grey and stark amid encircling trees. A rushing stream and weir were spanned by a rotting bridge whose timbers creaked under her feet.

She turned to look downstream into the depths of the millpool and her heart turned to ice inside her. There was a drumming in her ears, her lungs strained for breath, as if the dark waters were rising from their bed and closing over her.

There before her, pool, trees, everything in sight, were precisely as she had pictured them in 'Doom-water.' It was her painting come to life.

Chapter Eleven

Charlotte did not see Ker again for several days. Over the phone he spoke mysteriously of a special project; 'Tell you later,' was all he would say.

Yet she barely listened to him, for her mind was on Harford Mill. Her experience on that old bridge haunted her, awake or asleep, fear and fascination gripping her in turn.

Trying to put Harford Mill from her disturbed thoughts she turned to portrait work – Ker's, not Conrad's. But the mill's fascination was stronger.

Two days later she was back, carrying her gear through the park and heading for the millpond and its gloomy fringe of trees.

Excitement carried her on to the bridge. She would set up her easel looking down at the water from the exact viewpoint she had chosen in her imagination. Maybe if she could paint that scene again, it would turn out differently. Maybe she could exorcise the terrors which lay deep below the surface.

But the moment she stepped on to the crumbling timbers, the bridge began to shake as if alive, swaying with each step. The trembling under her feet set up an answering tremor in her whole being.

Before she reached halfway Charlotte was gripped by that sensation she had felt so many times before: blood drumming in her head, breath tight in her chest and the dark waters rising to draw her down. Only by force of will could she keep hold of her painting gear and step by step retreat to the safety of the ground.

Yet, she could not let herself be defeated. The very thing that terrified her would not let her leave the spot. But she knew that there was no way she could paint from the middle of the bridge. Still, she could cross over to the open ground beneath the grey, gaunt tower of the Old Mill and paint from there.

Gathering up her gear Charlotte began again. And again the shaking, gripping, freezing terror took hold, fixing her feet to the timbers beneath her. Slowly her eyes were drawn to the black, still depths beyond the foaming waters of the millrace. Her hold on paints, easel, the bridge-rail, began to slacken. She was sliding down, down.

'Are you all right, Charlotte?'

The voice behind her broke the spell. She pulled herself round. Angela, in tweed jacket and slacks, stood at the end of the bridge, sharp eyes alive with concern – or curiosity?

Angela strode on to the bridge, setting the planks shaking, 'Let me help you. You don't want to lose your paints.'

She took Charlotte's arm and together they edged to the mill side of the bridge. Angela said, 'This whole set-up will go downriver one day. I've warned Conrad.'

Once safely on the rough grass, Charlotte felt strength and normality return. 'I'm sorry,' she said. 'I don't know what happened. I just couldn't move.'

Angela looked at her without speaking for a moment. 'This is a strange place,' she said, after a pause. 'Wouldn't be surprised if it was haunted. Some poor thing drowned herself in the pool, I expect.'

'Don't!' gasped Charlotte.

'Sorry. Only joking. Like to see inside?'

Angela pushed on the mill door which opened with a groan. Inside was one huge chamber reaching up to cobwebbed rafters. The floor had been newly covered with raw, fresh planks; the windows, cleared of their old frames, were open, letting in the sunlight.

'Conrad's having this place fitted up for some special project he's suddenly decided on, something he won't discuss – with me, at least. Still, it's his money.'

'Would he mind my coming in here to paint?' asked Charlotte.

'Don't see why. I'm sure he wouldn't mind – at least until they start work here. I can ask him, if you like.'

'Is he here today?' Charlotte tried to keep her voice light, but Angela looked at her quickly.

'No. Now you see him, now you don't. He leaves me in charge most days.'

'That's a big responsibility.'

Angela shrugged. 'Conrad's quite sure of . . . his staff.' She paused, then, 'He chose people like himself.'

'How do you mean?'

'Why, orphans, people with no past, only futures – if you'll pardon the pun. It sounds strange . . .'

'I think that makes him special,' said Charlotte eagerly, and again Angela eyed her.

'Oh, Conrad's special all right. He always has

that effect on . . . people. But he's not easy to get close to.' Angela stopped, then deliberately went on, 'I've known him for nearly ten years – as well as anyone can.' A small smile played for a second round Angela's lips, then, 'There are things about him that baffle even me.'

Something in Angela's words, her tone, put Charlotte on her guard. But in that instant Angela's voice became light and chatty again.

'Look, Charlotte, you want to paint, not listen to me.'

Yes, she did want to paint and yes, she did want to hear more about Conrad Durrant. But she nodded and began to set up her easel. Angela watched her for a while, then abruptly turned away saying, 'Call in when you're finished – have a spot of lunch.'

Left alone, Charlotte worked. The view from the window was at an angle to the bridge. It took in the pool, the slope and a view of the house, through its screen of trees. Perhaps if she painted this view, then she might break the spell.

But no matter how she began, the aspect from the bridge kept its hold. Soon she saw she was painting 'Doomwater' all over again.

At last Charlotte gave up struggling, packed away her paints, folded her easel and left the mill.

This time she stood no nonsense from her crazy imagination. Clutching her gear tightly, she fixed her eyes on the slope ahead and marched over the bridge. The timbers swayed and cracked beneath her, but in five great strides she was over.

Ten minutes later she was in the large airy kitchen, at a yellow pine table, eating lunch with Angela. They chatted lightly about art and work, holidays, clothes.

Encouraged by the friendly atmosphere, Charlotte tried once more to question her about Conrad, but Angela avoided answering directly or simply changed the subject.

At last, sensing that Angela was not going to say any more about this young man she claimed to know so well, Charlotte got up to go.

'Better be off. Thanks for lunch, Angela. That was lovely.'

Angela rose, too. 'You're welcome.'

She walked out to the car with Charlotte and stood by while she loaded her gear and took her seat at the wheel. Then, just as Charlotte fastened her seat belt and was turning the key in the ignition, Angela leant her elbows on the open car window and spoke quietly but distinctly.

'Can I talk as a friend, Charlotte? Because despite what you think, I do like you.'

'But I don't . . .' Charlotte began. Angela went on, ignoring her protest.

'Look, I'm no fool. You are, shall we say, interested in Conrad. You may think I'm the jealous PA. Be my guest. But I'm going to say this anyway.

'I've seen Conrad take up with girls before – and drop them again. He's – like that.'

Stung, Charlotte cut in, 'Well, that's OK. You don't have any problem, do you?'

Angela took the words calmly. 'If it *were* like that, I *wouldn't* worry, believe me. But, since you – appeared – he's different. He's brooding about something. You are on his mind. And I . . . I don't think that's a good idea for him, or for you.'

Angela suddenly stood back from the car. 'I'm sorry, I've said enough.'

'A bit too much, I think,' said Charlotte coolly.

Angela raised both hands, like a flag of truce, 'Couldn't you just enjoy your painting here, without trying too hard to get inside Conrad's life?'

Charlotte bit her lip, started the engine. Then said, as calmly as she could, 'I think all that is between Conrad and me, don't you? Goodbye.'

As the car swept out into the drive she saw in the driving mirror, Angela, still standing there, hands clasped in front of her.

Chapter Twelve

Charlotte drove home, mind working furiously. She had been right. Angela was in love with Conrad and she had blundered into their lives. But what should she do – just back off? Perhaps Angela thought she had some claim on Conrad. But did he see it like that?

Charlotte drew up at the roundabout just outside town. Somehow there was more to Angela's words than 'keep off the grass', from one girl to another. She was hinting at something deeper. And there was something deeper for Charlotte, too, than boy-meets-girl.

In some way, Harford Mill with its dark pool and its new young owner, were linked as if by fate to the torment of her past five years. How and why she must know, whatever the answer, whatever the outcome.

A blast from a hooter behind her brought Charlotte back to reality. She drove on and put the thoughts away until she drew up at Gran's house.

She climbed the stairs to her studio and began to look for the half-finished sketch of Conrad. It was nowhere to be found, though she now began a careful search of the room.

Puzzled, she took up a sketchpad and began once more to block in the lines of Conrad's face. But now they were vague and elusive. She needed to see him again to be sure of the shape of the nose, the slant of the eyes, the angle of the jaw and the shape of that strange, intriguing scar.

She was still poring over her pad when there was a hesitant tap on her door. Ker's head poked in. 'May I?'

'I suppose so,' Charlotte mocked. 'We are not usually so shy, are we? What brought on this burst of good manners?'

Ker came in with both hands held up. Then he put the missing sketch of Conrad down on her desk. Charlotte sprang up, face white with an anger that surprised both of them.

'Go on, say I had no right,' he invited.

'Too right you didn't.' She snatched the sketch from him. 'I looked everywhere. What's going on,

Ker? I know we're friends, but this is a liberty.'

The corners of his mouth drooped at the force of her attack. Suddenly he looked not seventeen but seven. Then he recovered.

'Sorry, Charlie. I couldn't tell you why I borrowed it. You'd have taken off. I hoped I could put it back before you noticed.'

'Well,' she spoke carefully, 'you had better tell me why you borrowed it, then.'

He held out his other hand, revealing a sheet of photocopied paper, a newspaper cutting, a picture of a boy, maybe fifteen or sixteen. It was strangely familiar.

Taking the paper from Ker, Charlotte read the caption. "Darren Conway, teenage computer wizard who found himself in court this week on charges of fraud which a magistrate described as 'exceptional even in someone twice his age'." So? What's this got to do with anything?'

But she knew what. Under the anger her mind worked clearly. This was a younger Conrad. The scar on his unshaven chin was unmistakeable. So were the eyes. They looked out, wary, suspicious, defiant.

'Darren Conway,' said Ker. He tried to speak

formally but she could tell he was pleased with himself. 'They reckon when people change their names they never quite get rid of the old one. Superstition.'

'But how . . . ?' she began.

'I went through all our info on share dealing, future trading, stuff like that. I looked up some profiles of sensational young dealers. There are lots of them, graduating from Gameboy to Canary Wharf, from Sonic to stockbroker in two quick moves.

'But even in this league, Darren was ahead – brilliant. He was brought up in a children's home but he was fostered by a businessman and his wife . . .'

Ker halted in his story but Charlotte urged him to go on.

'The next bit isn't so heartwarming, Charlotte.'

'Go on!'

'They gave him everything, even wanted to adopt him. Filled his room with electronic gear. The foster-father had hopes of him taking over the business.'

'I bet.'

'Self-interest maybe. Or maybe he just wanted to give him a chance.'

'Go on, go on!'

'Little Darren was into the business already and the foster-dad didn't know. Money was being syphoned off and used for speculation. They found out how brilliant he was. In six months a million went downstream.

'And you know what he told the court?' Ker paused for effect.

Charlotte snapped, 'Tell me.'

' "Another week and I'd have got that lot back and then some",' Ker quoted.

'So? He was doing what they all do – and get a big hand for,' Charlotte interrupted.

'OK, Charlie. But usually they have permission to play with the dosh in the first place.'

'So, what are you telling me, Saint Matthew?'

'Don't be like that. I am just giving you the facts. You've met this Conrad Durrant and you think he's the business . . .'

'I never said a word . . .'

'You don't need to, Charlie. I am just telling you. He's brilliant. Maybe going straight. But a changed name means something dodgy. So, watch it, is what I say.'

'Thanks, Grandad.'

'Be like that. Anyway, can't stop. See you around.'

She did not answer. Ker stood for a moment, eyeing her anxiously, then shrugged and left the room.

Charlotte looked at the photocopy, then at her sketch and back again. She had not even noticed that Ker was gone. She was thinking, thinking . . .

Conrad Durrant, Darren Conway. Why, why did she have this feeling that she knew him already?

Chapter Thirteen

Charlotte passed a restless, sleepless night, but by morning her mind was made up. She rang Harford Mill. As she expected, Angela answered. When she asked to speak to Conrad, there was a moment's chill silence.

'He's very busy.'

'I know, but it's important I talk to him.'

Another silence. 'I'm not sure he'll like it . . .'

Charlotte felt anger well up inside her. 'Shall I come over without asking him then?'

Her tone, if not the words, had the desired effect.

'Just one moment,' Angela was formal now. A button was pressed, silence, then Conrad's voice, warm and natural.

'Hi, Charlotte. Of course. Come and share my coffee break. Eleven OK? Right, look forward to it.'

Charlotte glanced at the battered alarm clock by her bed. Ten o'clock already. She looked down at herself and then quickly peeled off the paint-stained T-shirt and jeans.

From her wardrobe she drew out a dress she had not worn yet – bought with the change from the car purchase, as she told herself at the time. She examined herself in the mirror. Too formal? No, she wanted that.

In the car she ran over the things which Ker had told her, refusing to make allowances for Conrad, looking at the worst case. This she divided into several questions. They sounded blunt, even offensive. But she needed to know the answers, whether they suited her or not. And if the questions did not suit Conrad, well that would be a sort of answer.

Conrad Durrant/Darren Conway had moved too far into her life for her not to know the truth, the whole truth. Something told her, though, that whatever the case, she was going to get to know Conrad better.

Everything that had happened so far fitted those predictions so exactly. But Charlotte also knew that the month of the horoscope was moving into its uncertain phase, when knowing the truth was more than important, it was vital.

What Ker had told her added up to bad news. She could turn the car round, turn her back on Harford

Mill and its eerie water, cut it out of her life. But she drove on.

Conrad was waiting on the steps. He took her hand and held it up while his eye ran over her dress.

'I like,' he said.

'Thank you, sir,' she answered.

Then his voice became brisk. 'Let's go round to the garden and have our coffee there. It's totally private.'

Something in his tone made Charlotte more alert. From the corner of her eye she saw a movement by the office door. Someone, Angela? had watched that little scene.

Once in the garden they sat at a white table in the shade of an enormous shrub with deep red flowers. A girl in white served coffee and cakes. Conrad nodded, 'Help yourself. I never eat during the day. Make a pig of myself at nightfall.'

He poured coffee then said, 'Right, about Darren Conway.'

Charlotte's mouth fell open. He smiled like a boy who has pulled off a conjuring trick unaided for the first time.

'How did you . . . ?' she began.

'That's how I make my bread. You coming out here meant you wanted to tell, or to ask me, something important. Right?'

'Still . . . ?'

'Look, when you've a big secret in your life you don't have to be paranoid to guess that people will try and find out. In fact, there's another trick of the trade. When you need to find things out, you are quick to spot when someone else is at the same game. I had a tip-off that someone was looking into my past.'

'Conrad,' Charlotte interrupted, 'you don't think that was me?'

'You?' He almost laughed, then resumed his serious expression. 'No, that is not your style. Your weakness is taking people on trust. It was your friend, Matthew, wasn't it?'

She nodded.

'He's good. I could use someone like him here, but I don't think he likes my style.'

Conrad looked at her again. She was taken aback by the way his eyes could switch from wary shyness to intense, almost piercing sharpness.

'What *do* you know about me, then?'

Charlotte breathed deeply, then slowly repeated everything Ker had told her. Conrad nodded and said simply, 'Those are the facts, but not the whole truth. My foster-father did have hopes of me. His evidence got me probation and community service, rather than anything more serious. He wanted me, and the money, back. I gave him one, but not the other. It took me another year but I paid him back every penny, then said goodbye.

'There and then I swore I'd work for myself alone. And since I didn't want that "whizz kid in court" tag any more, I arranged a new identity. Secrecy is possible in the information age, if you know how.'

He leaned forward, put a hand on her arm. 'I've outgrown Darren Conway.' His hand moved away towards the beard. 'I *am* Conrad Durrant now. I look forward, not back.'

He watched as she drained her coffee cup.

'Charlotte. You're going to pass judgement. That's important to me. But before you do, I'd like to show you something which may surprise you even more than this. It may help you to decide if you want to know me any more.'

Chapter Fourteen

Conrad led the way from the walled garden down towards the mill. As they left the belt of trees and came out into the open, Charlotte stopped in surprise.

The shores of the millpool swarmed with men. The quiet of the place was broken by hammering and sawing. She took a quick glance at Conrad and saw, just as quickly, that boyish gleam of pride come and go like a spark in his eyes.

On the bridge, Charlotte paused to take hold of her feelings. She looked down to hide her face. But Conrad seemed to misunderstand her hesitation.

'Take my hand,' he urged, 'I know this bridge isn't safe, may give way at any moment. But no point in repairing it. I'm going to have a new one built in traditional stone. Come.'

He took her hand and drew her swiftly over to the other side. Now the door to the mill swung open noiselessly. Inside more men worked, painting walls, plastering the high, domed ceiling. Already the window overlooking the water had been replaced, an enormous ornamental sill added. Outside, bushes had been cleared to give a wider view of the house on the rise.

'It's fantastic,' murmured Charlotte.

Conrad spoke briefly to one of the men and all of them left their work and went outside. He turned to Charlotte.

'Hoped you'd say that, because I – I'd like your approval for what I'm planning.'

'Mine?' She stared.

'Yes, as an artist. I know it sounds boring but I intend to turn Harford Mill into a gallery.'

'A gallery?'

'Right. It sounds as though I'm doing a copycat on Saatchi, but it's my own thing. You see, Charlotte, I'm making my way, fast. I'm not bragging when I say I'm going up like a rocket. And I want other young people to rise with me.'

He took her by the arms. 'I know Angela told you about the orphan bit. Well, I'm not being sentimental. I want *us* to show *them*, the ones who think they've got it all nailed down, that we are coming through. You do see, don't you?'

'Yes, yes. But why me?'

He was almost shaking her in his urgency. 'Because you are special. You are obsessed.'

'Me?' How much did he know? Ice formed inside Charlotte, then melted again as he went on.

'Your painting. You are not going to be just good. You are going to be great.'

'But, Conrad, how? How did . . . ?'

'Don't say anything, just listen. I told you I'd something more to tell you. Call it a confession, though I'm not ashamed . . . our meeting, it wasn't chance – '

'Not chance?'

'Don't get me wrong. I don't mean destiny. Things happen because you make them happen. Dreams come true because you shape them. So, Charlotte, I fixed it so we'd meet, I decided I must meet you, when . . .'

'Decided? What do you mean, Conrad?'

He turned and took hold of a cord that hung down below a curtain on the wall. Charlotte cried out as the curtain drew aside to reveal a painting.

Conrad spoke triumphantly. 'The first picture in my Gallery of the Future. "Doomwater".'

Chapter Fifteen

'You told him?'

Ker's face across the café table was pink with outrage and incredulity. Charlotte had arranged to meet him here in the hope that they could have a calm, non-personal discussion, not a shouting match. One look at Ker's expression told her she was mistaken.

But she spoke calmly, willing him to be reasonable, to understand.

'I had to know. I had to find out from him. If I am to go on . . .' she had nearly said, 'seeing Conrad', but changed it to, 'painting at Harford Mill, I had to know the truth.'

Ker shook his head as if in pity. 'And you think a guy with his track record is into telling the truth?'

'As it happens, Ker, I do. For one thing he agreed everything you found out was true.'

'He could hardly deny it.'

Charlotte ignored the interruption and went on,

'He gave more details. How much he – took – and how he paid it back and . . .'

'And you believed him.'

Charlotte gritted her teeth and hissed at Ker, 'All right, Mr Investigator. Check it out. You're good at checking on people.'

'Thank you. It's my job. I'm not ashamed of it.'

She retorted, 'And making money's his job. There are good and bad in every line of business.'

'And he's one of the good brigade?'

'He told me everything.'

'Everything?' Ker started to laugh.

'Shut up and listen.' Charlotte's voice rose. Ker listened.

'You were right about him, Ker, twice. His track record for one. And for another, it was him who bought my picture for his new gallery.'

'I see,' said Ker. 'I'm right every time and you still think he's wonderful?'

'I never said that.' Charlotte's face was pink.

'Not much. You must think I'm stupid. You're going over the top about a bloke you met all of ten days ago.'

'Why not? These things do happen.'

'In a pig's ear. That stupid horoscope predicted love at first sight and you go along with it as if you'd got nothing between your ears.'

'Ker! What is this trip? Why should it matter so much to you?'

Ker lifted his coffee cup, saw it was empty and put it down with a clatter. 'Because for all these cosy confessions, Mr Darren Conway Conrad Durrant, or whatever names he may use on Sundays, is economical with the truth.'

'How?'

'He employs orphans. Big deal. Angela and little Darren were in the same children's home. So are other people at Harford Mill. And they all have form, that's how.'

Silenced for a moment, Charlotte spat out, 'We are digging the dirt, aren't we? What else? Did he murder his parents?'

Ker made a face. 'If you want the details. Father unknown. Mother a drug addict. Abandoned him. He doesn't even know her name, nor does anyone else. Conway's a hand-out name. Doesn't even know when he was born. That's why he's not into birth signs.'

Birth signs. Suddenly Charlotte saw the scar on

the chin of the young Darren, more clearly than before. Then the insight was overwhelmed by her rage.

'Why are you telling me all these rotten things?' she demanded, white-faced.

Ker's voice was tight with controlled anger, 'He's had a raw deal. He's got a lot to escape from. He's had to make his life up as he goes along. A fantasist or worse.'

He pushed his chair back and stood up. 'Feel sorry for him. I would. But trust him, go along with him? No. He's trouble, Charlie. Maybe danger. There, I've told you.'

Now she was on her feet, 'You've known me a long time, Ker, but you are not running my life.'

'Don't worry,' he answered. 'From now I stay out of it.'

Turning his back he marched out. The slam of the door as he left made people stare at Charlotte as, biting her lip, she left too.

Chapter Sixteen

For two days Charlotte did nothing, paralysed by her conflicting feelings. Years of warm, easy friendship with Ker where every argument was fun, had broken up in a violent row, the first and, maybe, the last.

Ker's anger was so unexpected, so unlike him. In the past he had always been calm, sceptical, full of common sense. She could bounce her problems off him and get answers.

But never before had any disagreement been so personal. Conrad was danger, he'd said, but go your own way. He was warning her and washing his hands of her at the same time.

She picked up the predictions from her desk. She knew the words by heart: '. . . *great rush of self-confidence will carry you on, ignoring friendly warnings which, rather than steadying you, will only provoke you . . . All will now be risk and confusion.*

'Who can you trust? . . . As a new, exciting

relationship develops, must an old, tried and trusted one be shattered?'

Who can you trust? In the depths of her mind, she knew somehow that she had decided, it was decided for her, but still she felt rooted to the spot in time and space like someone in a dream.

The phone rang, bringing her to her feet with a jolt. It was Angela.

'Charlotte? If you're free this weekend, Conrad's throwing a party – well, a few friends, people he wants to do deals with. But don't bother with that. You're invited to come and paint – please yourself.'

'Er, thanks . . . I . . .' Charlotte's hesitation was quickly picked up by Angela.

'Of course, if you'd rather not . . . if you have other plans . . .'

Was Angela speaking for Conrad, or herself? There was just a trace, a hint of – stay away? – in her voice. But it was enough to decide Charlotte.

'I'd love to.'

'Terrific!' Angela was back in her PA mode. She went on, 'And Conrad says, "Bring your clever friend," and stay over, right?'

'Right.'

Charlotte put the phone down and stared out of the window. Bring my clever friend, who thinks I am an idiot and my host is evil.

Should she pass the message on? Come and be my chaperone? Rub salt in it? Really insult Ker?

Downstairs, she heard Gran clattering in the kitchen. Noise was her way of saying, 'Why do I have to bother with housework?' The sounds suddenly put Charlotte at ease.

She went down into the kitchen. Gran took one look at her face then pointed to the table.

'Sit down. Don't say a word. Five minutes.'

Five minutes later two plates of spaghetti bolognese were slapped on to the table. Chianti gurgled into two glasses. Gran took a mouthful of wine then said, 'I am all ears.'

When Charlotte had finished talking, Gran's plate and glass were empty. 'That's better. I hate cooking but I can't think on an empty stomach.' She poured another glass for herself then looked at Charlotte.

'Have you fallen for what's-his-name at Harford Mill?' She paused. 'Harford Mill rings bells . . . We used to go there for picnics. The owner then didn't mind . . .'

Charlotte stopped eating, fork in the air, the spaghetti slowly unwinding. Suddenly there was a drumming in her ears, green water was drawing her down, down.

Gran leaned over and gently lowered Charlotte's hand. 'You'll have it all in your lap, love. Never mind Memory Lane. The future's what counts. I stopped you answering my question.'

'I don't know, Gran. I'm mixed-up.'

'What, about him?'

'Oh, I think he likes me. But it's my art he's really interested in.'

Gran started to laugh, then put a hand to her mouth. 'Sorry, love, just my twisted mind. But I'll tell you one thing. Matthew may be jealous, you know.'

'Ker, jealous? Oh, Gran!'

'That young man cares a lot about you, Charlie. But you don't see it behind all those jokes and mock battles over ideas . . .'

'Gran,' said Charlotte in a small voice. 'You're just making me feel rotten.'

'Look, Charlie. Love can be like that. A loves B, but B loves C. Can't be helped.'

'But how can you know for sure?'

'You don't know for sure, to start off with. You find out.'

She leaned across the table and took Charlotte's hand. 'I'll tell you something that perhaps I shouldn't. When your mother met your father, she thought he was handsome, brilliant, fantastic. I thought different. But it was her life. Later she found out he wasn't *so* brilliant. I'm afraid it was my money that kept the show on the road. We're lucky to still have this house.'

'Oh, Gran. You never said . . .'

'Why should I? My decision. The point is, when your mother found out your father wasn't what he seemed, she'd already found out something else. She loved him. That's the point. When you love someone, you know. That's what counts. Finding out is the name of the game. It may take time, it may not. But, Charlie, love. It takes nerve.'

Chapter Seventeen

Saturday dawned fresh and fine. But by mid-morning the heat was building up. The weekend was going to be a scorcher – the perfect setting for Harford Mill.

Charlotte was excited inside herself as she packed her overnight bag and assembled brushes, canvasses. Yet her movements were slow and reluctant. Part of her was eager, part was hanging back and she knew why.

As she made coffee and sat at her desk, the sentence from the horoscope repeated in her mind . . . '*As a new, exciting relationship develops, must an old, tried and trusted one be shattered*?'

Was this prediction uncannily accurate or was she acting out an episode in her own life that had been scripted for her by an unknown hand? Each step carried her into the unknown and exciting, away from the familiar, the certain.

She wanted to get away from the past. But did that mean leaving Ker behind? Maybe you had to accept that you gained and you lost. But why should she lose Ker just because of Conrad?

Gran had warned her Ker might be jealous. But she couldn't see him like that, mean and petty. Yet in that row in the café she had been just as angry. She had rejected Ker. He wasn't her keeper. Yet she'd been insulting, accused him of muck-raking. She'd been unreasonable.

Twice Charlotte reached out for the phone to call Ker and say, 'Hey, this is stupid, isn't it?' But she hadn't done it. In between she'd half-listened for the phone to ring. But it hadn't. No olive branch from his side of the barricade.

Should she ring him now – pass on Conrad's invitation? He didn't mind Ker being around, even though Ker had nosed into his past. He seemed totally laid back about Ker. Maybe that was because he was totally laid back about her. Maybe all this didn't matter to him one little bit. Maybe all this was in her head, like the horoscope, like the dark mill waters, like nightmares of sun, sea and consuming fire.

The thoughts rushed through her head like a train in a tunnel, bringing a great bolt of pain between her eyes. The space in front of her grew dark. Desperate, she stood up and reached for the phone. Yet she could not ring Ker. She dreaded his hostility to Conrad, his contempt, because somehow, now, they seemed aimed at her.

No, she must leave well alone. Ker must go his way, she hers. Ten years was too long for a childhood friendship. She had to make a fresh start.

She bent down and checked the overnight bag, zipped it up and began to pick up her painting gear. She was loaded like a pack-horse, but she couldn't bear to make two journeys up and down the stairs. Get going, Charlotte.

There was a footstep on the landing. She put down her bag. Her heart suddenly thumped. Gran was out, wasn't she?

Her door slowly opened. Into the gap poked a stick. At the end hung a handkerchief, not exactly clean, but definitely once white. Behind it a familiar voice said, 'Can I come in?'

'Ker, you idiot,' squealed Charlotte. 'Of course.'

The familiar ugly face followed the flag of truce. Ker carried a canvas holdall. 'Had a phone call from Angela – come for a dirty weekend at Harford Mill. I thought if I grovelled, you'd give me a lift.'

'Stupid. Course I will. I'm so glad you're coming. Hey, I'm sorry . . .'

'Oh, shut up,' Ker said. 'So am I. Forget it. Let's go.'

Chapter Eighteen

As they drove through the country lanes towards Harford Mill, Charlotte's earlier mood of desperation gave way to one of relief, of excitement, like a child before a party. A small voice told her, 'It's going to be all right. It's going to be good.'

Ker urged on her mood with jokes, idiotic guesses at what the cows in the fields were thinking, caustic comments on the farmyard smells, 'Get away from the polluted cities into the fresh air of the countryside. Who are they kidding?'

He thrust his arm out of the open side window and beat on the car door, singing, 'We're off to see the Wizard, the wonderful Wizard of Dosh.'

'Knock it off, Ker,' begged Charlotte, giggling. 'You'll have me off the road.'

'Right,' he said, drawing in his arm. 'Hey, look, I'm sunburnt already. How's about I stick my leg out next?'

'You do that and the rest of you goes out.'

'Aye, aye, Skipper!'

'Anyway, you can lie in the sun all day,' she went on. 'Some of us have to work.'

'No, Ma'am,' answered Ker. 'No sunbathing this weekend. The smoke-filled rooms for me. With luck some of Conrad's little friends can tell me a thing or two . . .'

'Will they talk to you, like that?'

'Yeah. Off the record. All manic experts are the same. Nothing they like better than talking shop.'

A sudden anxiety gripped Charlotte, 'Hey, Ker, you're not going to ask . . .'

'Give over,' he answered with sudden force. 'I am not, repeat not, going to probe the murky Durrant past. That file is closed. You want to find out more, that's your affair.'

'I don't know.' Charlotte tried to keep her voice light. 'I just have this feeling I've met him before.'

'No, kid.' Ker's voice grew colder. 'He's a type. Tall, dark, etc. TV actor, like that.' He paused, then said sharply, 'If you're that curious why not ask him? At this stage in the game he can't take it as a come-on.'

'What game?' She eyed Ker in the driving mirror.

'Oh grow up, Charlie. You're keen on the bloke so you find out more. I'm not so I won't.'

They sat in uneasy silence for a while, then Ker said, 'Hey, here we are.'

Charlotte came down to earth from a reverie about Conrad as they swung into the drive, the gatekeeper waving them on. Cars already filled the space before the main doors. Arnold, still in uniform, was directing drivers to parking spaces.

Angela waved to them from the top of the steps. 'Hi. Conrad's in a boring old meeting till the afternoon. But I've got a lunch box for you, Charlotte, if you want to paint. Matthew gets to lunch in the kitchen with me while we talk market prices.'

She ran down the steps and helped Charlotte unload the car. 'Guess what? We're having a barbecue by the lake, late afternoon sometime.' Angela's voice was light, almost too easy, thought Charlotte. 'Look,' she went on, 'I'll take your bag up to your room, so that you can get out there and paint.'

Then, to Charlotte's astonishment, Angela took Ker's arm and led him away. 'Some people you might like to meet, Matthew.'

At the foot of the steps Charlotte watched them

go into the house together, chattering. It seemed they'd forgotten her already. Despite herself, she felt piqued.

But in half an hour she had begun to recover her good mood as she worked at her easel on the slope over the millpool. On the open turf outside the shade of the trees, the sun shone down with such force that she was glad she had swapped T-shirt and jeans for loose top and skirt.

At first she concentrated on a view of the house, its yellow stone glowing in the noonday sun. Then suddenly feeling hungry, she sat down under the trees and opened the lunch box – chicken legs, salmon pâté, orange in a chill bag.

Her meal finished, she stood up. The happy mood of the morning was growing into a kind of boldness. Abruptly she decided to put an end to the nonsense in her mind. 'Doomwater' was a work of art, not a destiny. The predictions were wrong, weren't they? Her friendship with Ker wasn't shattered by whatever-was-to-be with Conrad. And, right at this moment, her future was in her hands. She would paint what she liked, when and where she chose.

The urgency of her thoughts carried her down the

slope, painting gear gathered up in her arms. The grey tower of the mill came into view, new windows sparkling in the sun. The work was finished it seemed and the men had gone away.

A few more strides and she was at the old bridge. Drawing together her armful of painting gear, so that she could pass through the narrow space between the rails, she set foot on the planks.

As she did a tremor ran through the whole structure. Now she had both feet on and the tremor grew to a trembling and shaking, as if the mouldering timbers had a life of their own.

Willpower drove her on, feet stamping in an effort to carry her over. With each stride, the swaying grew. Overhead, trees cut out the sun, the air was suddenly chill and the chill invaded her body. Below her the waters from the sluice swirled darkly.

They seemed to rise up, calling her, drawing her down. Vainly Charlotte tried to command her legs to go forward. Her head began to spin, her mind to empty of conscious thought.

Her easel dropped with a clatter. Blindly she reached out with the free hand, grasping the rotting rail. With a sickening crack it snapped, her knees buckled and she began to crumple and fall, as the black depths rose up to claim her.

Chapter Nineteen

Far above her was an arch of gleaming white stretching into infinity. In her ears was the distant roar of falling water. Slowly her scattered senses returned. She was looking up at the newly plastered ceiling of the mill. She moved her head. A blade of pain drove into her.

'Keep still please, Charlotte.'

Conrad's face appeared. His deep-set eyes gazed into hers, 'It's all right. Keep still.'

She tried to sit up. He put his arm round her shoulders. Her body relaxed, the pain died to an ache.

'What happened?' she asked.

'My fault, entirely.' His voice was almost humble. 'I should have had that contraption repaired or pulled down. As soon as the blokes come back on Monday it's going – for firewood.'

'But – how?'

'Something made me leave the meeting and come down here. Don't ask me what. I just felt I had to get down to the mill. As I came down the slope, I saw the rail break. Your head hit the timbers – I ran and luckily I grabbed you as you were slipping into the water.'

'But, my . . . ?'

'Your gear's almost OK. The bad news is the easel went into the pool.'

'Oh.' Charlotte tried to struggle up from the couch on which she lay, but he held her still.

'Look, we'll try and fish it out later. Meanwhile, the good news is . . .'

He waved towards the broad window. There stood a new easel, not unlike hers but of finer wood, with shining brass fittings.

Laughing at her amazement, he said, 'That's yours. I had it brought in yesterday.'

'Mine, Conrad? I couldn't,' she protested.

'You have to. It was intended as a – well – a bargaining counter. Now you'd better have it as an out-of-court settlement, so you don't sue me over that bridge.'

'Bargaining counter? I don't understand . . .'

'There was a condition attached. But after this débâcle, who am I to make conditions?'

Charlotte tried to stand up. At first she swayed while Conrad's arm supported her. She looked round. The room was now decorated and furnished with tables and chairs in a light, elegant wood.

She drew out of his grasp and faced him. She stared. His face was changed. Then she realised. The beard . . .

'What condition? And why have you shaved off your beard?'

He did not smile at the confusion of her questions. His eyes were fixed on hers.

'The condition was that you paint my portrait.'

'But, I'd do that anyway, Conrad. Gladly. I wanted to. No need to bargain. But . . .'

'The beard? Well, I thought that now you know my past, no point in concealment. So I shaved it off.'

While he talked her eyes were on his face, the line of his jaw. The scar, faintly seen in the old press picture, now stood out, white against the tan of his cheeks. It was a curious scar, too regular to be accidental. It was like a letter M, with a satanic tail curving up from the third down-stroke.

It was unmistakeable. Scorpio. And with that came

the answer to her question. She was rushing headlong through time, to another place, other water, another sun, but the same two people facing one another.

She knew where she had met Conrad before.

Chapter Twenty

'Charlotte? Have you seen a ghost?'

Yes, she had. But she answered quickly, 'No. Just thinking what might have happened – out there.'

He spoke just as quickly. 'Stupid of me. Look, let's get away from here, right now.'

Taking her arm he led her from the mill, carefully drew her across the bridge with its broken rail and up the slope towards the house. The sky over them was steely blue. In the open the heat was stunning. Conrad talked easily to distract her.

'Never mind the gear. It can stay there – like till tomorrow – maybe for the first portrait session.'

Then he stopped and faced her. 'Stupid again. You won't want to go near that place tomorrow. Selfishly, I was just thinking of my portrait in that gallery-to-be.'

Charlotte heard her voice rise, 'I want to go back, Conrad. I can't let a stupid accident put me off.'

'Sure?'

'Sure I'm sure,' she answered and knew she was lying. Seen a ghost? She had done more than see a ghost, she had caught a glimpse of the past. It was as though a curtain had been drawn back, letting in harsh light. Things, people in deep shadow, once invisible, now stood out starkly.

She knew exactly where she had seen this strange young man with the Scorpio sign etched into the skin of his jaw. And knowing brought to her such a torrent of feeling she could neither think nor talk straight.

But Conrad, who had triggered this emotion . . . she could not tell him yet. The person at the centre of this turmoil inside her, she could not talk to him about it.

Yet she had to tell someone. And there was only one person she could talk to – Ker. But would he listen? Dare she speak to him?

They were entering the house, Conrad's arm still round her shoulders. A small group of men in suits turned curiously to look at them. But two people, deep in conversation at a table in the corner, ignored them. Angela and Ker, so close their heads almost touched.

They drew apart almost guiltily as Conrad spoke, voice raised, 'Listen everyone. Charlotte's had a bit of an accident at that stupid bridge. My fault. She needs to lie down . . .'

'I'm OK, now, honestly,' Charlotte began. But Conrad continued as if she'd not spoken.

'We won't start the barbecue until she's had time to rest. OK?'

Now he looked down at her. 'Angela will go upstairs with you, and don't come down till you're OK. You have to be fit for,' he paused, 'tomorrow.'

He drew her closer, kissed her lightly, then stood away. Now everyone was staring at her. Angela, mouth tight, stepped towards her.

'Come on, Charlotte. I'll take you up to your room.'

Though the touch on her arm was gentle, something made Charlotte throw it off. She sidestepped Angela and turned to Ker, lowering her voice.

'I must talk to you, alone, now.'

His answer was neutral. 'Charlie. You look shaken up. You need to lie down. Let's talk another time, later . . .'

'Not later, please, Ker,' she insisted. 'Something I've just remembered.' Now she was whispering. 'Something about Conrad.'

His voice grew colder. 'I don't think you really want to do that, Charlotte. You're upset.'

She grew excited, but tried to keep her voice low. 'It's from that time – five years back.'

Now Ker raised his voice, 'No, Charlie. What you need is rest.'

'Ker. It's important.'

'It seems like that now, Charlie. But when you've rested, it won't.' His controlled irritation now triggered anger in her.

'Don't you understand, Ker?'

'Yes, I do.' Now everyone in the room could hear. 'I thought we'd agreed to forget all – that. I don't want to hear any more about your trips down the Time Tunnel. Not interested – read my lips.' He started to walk away.

'Ker!'

Charlotte's head spun, her eyes blurred. She sensed they were all staring at her. She was creating a scene.

Angela took her arm again, firmly. 'Matthew's right. After that business at the bridge, you need to rest.'

The pain in her head was now so violent it almost blinded her. Weak with nausea, Charlotte felt Angela guide her up the broad staircase, along the passage and into a bedroom.

She lay on the bed, and a damp cloth was pressed to her burning forehead. It must be Angela but she could see no one. It might all be a dream.

In that dream a voice said gently, coaxingly, 'Charlotte, if you'd like to go home, away from all this, Arnold can drive you there. I'll come with you. It might be better.'

From somewhere Charlotte drew strength to turn her back. The door closed quietly. Though somewhere on the edge of her dream she seemed to hear Ker and Angela whispering about her.

Then the sounds died. She was alone, alone with her memories and their pain, the distress of Ker's hostility, the sick ache in her head. She felt herself sink into hopelessness as into deep, dark water, down, down, down . . .

Chapter Twenty-one

Maybe she slept, maybe her trance-like state blotted out all sense of time. But a noise made Charlotte open her eyes. The twilight of the bedroom was pierced by a shaft of light, throwing a yellow patch on to the dark wall near her bed.

A wind was sweeping up the hill from the pool, stirring the slats of the Venetian blinds. As they turned in the breeze, light and shade followed one another.

A distant mutter of thunder, from below voices, laughter, the sound of glasses and plates, the scent of grilling meat wafted on hot air. Light, sound, smell, all took Charlotte into another time span.

She was back in the villa on Santa Vittoria, lying on the bed, racked by a sick, angry headache and her rage with her father.

The blinds rattled, turned, and in the lit space on the wall she saw her parents' faces, father's red with fury, mother's pale, calm, eyes anxious. So clear was the image it brought Charlotte up from her bed. Then she sank down again, the head pain blotting out all sensible thought.

She could only think, feel and be as she was then, twelve years old, desperate with heat and anger.

Again a rumble of thunder, closer, the stormless thunder of a heatwave. A rush of wind, a waft of cooking meat, laughter, a cork popping, knives, forks, plates. Snatches of conversation . . . her name, 'Charlotte . . . wait.'

The blinds turning, another shaft of light and the film began again. Her parents walking out, her mother with one last, pleading glance, her father not even turning his head. She, tied to the bed by her anger as surely as if lashed with ropes.

Dark, light. Below – at Harford Mill or on Santa Vittoria? – a car engine started. Her parents were going, to their deaths. She knew this with the then-now certainty of a dream. Driving away to their deaths, down the ravine, bounding, turning over, the car bouncing like a toy, exploding, burning, burning.

'We won't wait for ever.'

It was real now, not a dream, and with it came the sound of Charlotte's scream, again and again.

She was snatching at the door, but could not open

it, scrabbling at the wood, vainly seeking the handle.

'Charlotte! What's wrong?'

Conrad was there, in the passage, holding her close, murmuring.

'I was coming up to ask if you were OK to join us, when I heard you. What was it – a nightmare?'

'No, Conrad. It was real. I was back – when my parents died. I saw them. I heard my father's voice.' The tears streamed down her face.

He was kissing, comforting her, 'It's all right now. That was then. It's gone. You're here with me.'

'I want to stay with you, Conrad. Don't let me go back. Hold me,' she gasped.

His whisper stilled the shaking in her body. 'Don't worry. I won't let you go. This is for ever.'

Chapter Twenty-two

When Charlotte woke it was daylight. Outside the sky had changed from blue to pearly-white. Along the skyline purple clouds were massing. The heat was building up to a point where it would be unbearable. The air was alive with tension.

Yet Charlotte was calm. Her storm had passed. Today she was ready to take the tangled strands of her life and unravel them. Today, broken bridge or not, she would go to the mill. Conrad would join her and she would begin his portrait.

As she drew she would talk, tell him what she knew, what she remembered. Artists must know their subjects, her tutor had said. Now she understood as never before.

She knew Conrad. But before the portrait could be completed, he must know what she knew. There must be no secrets, no shadows between them. The future could begin only if the past was laid to rest.

Her disappointment was intense as she entered

the dining-room and saw no Conrad. Angela, talking to other guests, rose as Charlotte entered.

'You're better. It shows. You look rested. Come and sit down. I'll get you a coffee.'

The others nodded, smiled, went on talking to one another. Ker came into the room. He looked round urgently but his gaze passed over Charlotte. He was talking to Angela, quietly but distinctly.

'Have to go, Angela.'

'Oh, Ker!' The casual use of the nickname jolted Charlotte. 'Must you?'

'Sorry. My father's not well . . . last night. I have to go home.'

'That's bad. I'll call Arnold.'

'No need. Taxi's on its way. Anyway, thanks for everything. Tell Conrad, please.'

Impulsively Charlotte rose to go to Ker, but already he had left the room and she sank to her chair again.

Angela was beside her now, offering the coffee. 'What'll it be today, Charlotte? Mill's a no-go area after yesterday, I guess.'

Charlotte tensed. Was Angela asking her or telling her? Surely she wasn't imagining this. She was being warned off being with Conrad.

She answered quietly, firmly, 'Oh, I shan't let that stupid business stop me. I have – reasons for painting at the mill.' Angela could see hidden meanings in *that* if she liked.

There was a moment's silence which spread to other people at the table, then Conrad entered. As his eyes met Charlotte's, he smiled a quick, intimate smile, before he spoke to the room at large.

'Sorry folks, to be a bad host, but I'm in my room all this morning, maybe all day. Urgent business. So the 'don't disturb' sign is up, OK? See you all for a late lunch, maybe.'

His glance crossed Charlotte's again. He must have seen her sudden disappointment. He gave no sign. But maybe that was just his way. She bent over her coffee cup as he left the room.

Angela touched her arm. 'Hope you don't think I was trying to tell you where you ought to paint. I know better than that.'

Charlotte made herself smile. 'Doesn't matter, Angela. I haven't made my mind up, anyway.'

That was true, she thought as she left the dining-room. Her mind, trying to grasp too many things at once, couldn't get to grips with anything.

Ker's going had hurt her. But there was no middle way, was there? What she felt for Conrad, what she felt for Ker. Those two things could not mix. There was a cold jealousy in Ker's words and manner that she had never dreamed could come from him.

But it had. Ten years' friendship was gone, in days, hours, almost. As predicted.

Deep in thought, Charlotte wandered through the trees and down the slope. The air shimmered with heat. Dark clouds were edging up the sky while thunder growled, and in the strange light the still mill-pool gleamed like molten lead.

She halted at the bridge. A thin rope guarded the gap in the rail. It all seemed so long ago. Now she was calm. Nothing to fear – only her own fantasies. She was seventeen, not twelve. This was the long goodbye to tormented childhood. She was crossing over.

Ignoring the groans and shaking in the timber, walking lightly, staring straight ahead at the tall dark shape of the mill, she reached the grass on the other side.

Now the door swung open noiselessly. There was the gallery chamber, white and high, lit by a ray of sunshine shooting from behind the swarming thunder-clouds.

There was her easel, her painting gear stacked beneath it. There on the wall, curtain drawn back, was her 'Doomwater' picture.

And there, sitting on the couch, casually stroking his scarred chin, was Conrad.

Chapter Twenty-three

Conrad rose, grinning like a boy at Charlotte's astonishment. Now you see him, now you don't, Angela had said. As always he seemed to read her thoughts. He put a finger to his lips.

'Angela and the others think I'm in my hideaway – my work room where I am never, ever, disturbed. It's where I go when the market's in free fall and we have to shift everything round the world, but fast. That's where they think I am. But I'm not, I'm here, having my portrait painted, by you.'

Charlotte pretended to be put out. 'How do you know I'm not just here to paint the millpool? How did you even know I'd be here?'

'I knew you would.' Now his voice lost its chuckle. 'I know how you feel about water. I know how you fear it and how it draws you.' He gestured to the painting on the wall. 'Once the artist paints, the world knows all the secrets.'

Smiling to lighten his words he bent to open a

hamper on the floor. 'This is supposed to keep me going during my day's work, but it'll do for us both. We can stay here all day and no one will know where we are, or what we're doing.'

Flustered, Charlotte began to adjust the easel.

She tried to take charge – of him, of herself? 'Sit where you were on the couch,' she said, 'and smile as you did when I came in and found you here.' Then she added mockingly, 'As you do when you're pleased with yourself.'

'Oh, I'm self-satisfied, am I?'

'No,' she answered. 'It's just that all sorts of strange ideas seem to excite you. That makes you different. One moment I feel I know you, the next you're a mystery.'

'Mystery, secrets.' Conrad seated himself and ran his finger over the M-shaped scar, almost like a signal to her, the sign of a secret society. We know, don't we? But she was not ready for that, yet.

'I collect secrets, like some folk collect antiques,' went on Conrad. 'Is it OK for me to talk or does it spoil the pose?'

'I don't want you to pose, Conrad. I want you to let me see yourself, so talk.'

He bent and took out a bottle from the basket, then a glass. 'Drink?'

She shook her head. 'Can't drink and paint. Like driving.'

He laughed. 'Well, I shall.' He poured wine and drank as if thirsty. 'I knew you would come down to the mill, Charlotte, come what may. I know so much about you.

'It's an orphan's game, finding out. Your past is a secret. You have to know. I had to know where I came from . . . my parents. Knowing is the name of the game in my trade. That's why I make money, not because money means anything – rows of figures on a screen. But it means I know what other people don't know.'

Charlotte looked at the sketched outline in front of her. Conrad's lips were smiling but his eyes were not. They looked out from the canvas deep into hers. He was looking at her in the same way. It was disturbing, exciting. To cover her feelings she bent over the drawing, then said lightly, 'You stopped talking. Go on. Things you know that others don't.'

'Yes,' said Conrad. 'When I bought "Doomwater" I said you must not know who the buyer was. Then I sat in my car at the roundabout outside town and watched you drive past on the last day of term.'

The charcoal snapped in Charlotte's fingers. 'The silver limo. I remember now.'

'Right. I arranged our meeting. I knew where your car would stop. I knew you would think it was chance. I knew you would want to know more about me – but not the version your clever friend worked out. You didn't believe that, did you?'

Charlotte picked up a charcoal stick and looked at Conrad. Sunlight from the thundery sky outside lit his face. She felt dizzy and rested her hand on the edge of the easel.

'It wasn't that I didn't believe Ker,' she began slowly. 'He had the facts. I just . . . saw them in a different way. He thought they meant one thing, I thought they meant another.'

'And your version won, Charlotte. You chose your story, not his. It's not what happens that counts, it's what you believe.'

'Yes, Conrad. And I believe you, because – I know you and Ker does not.'

She was coming closer to it.

'Yes, Charlotte,' he murmured. 'Ker has gone,

hasn't he. Angela's not here. Now, it's just you and me.'

As Conrad spoke the still hot air was stirred by a breeze and thunder crashed around the mill.

'Our story, Charlotte. Your story and mine.'

Chapter Twenty-four

Charlotte put down the charcoal and walked to the couch where Conrad sat. Picking up the empty glass she held it out. Silently he poured wine and watched as she sat down, half-turned to face him. She was close enough to touch him, but first she must speak.

'Since my parents died, Conrad, everything else that happened that summer has blanked out in my mind, like a door slamming. Nothing mattered – just them dying.'

He nodded.

'When Ker brought me that old newspaper picture of Darren Conway I did not remember the name. But that scar on the chin . . . I knew I'd seen that before.

'The funny thing was he showed me that picture to warn me about you, to put me off.'

Charlotte sipped the dry cool wine. Conrad smiled, waiting.

'But it just made me want to know more about

you. It told me I knew you already. Like a door opening a crack to let in light.

'At first I thought I was fantasising – I'd known you in another existence, in a dream. But I knew there was more. I knew it was from – five years ago. But I could not see past my parents' deaths.

'When you saved me at the bridge, and asked me to paint your portrait, I saw you had shaved off your beard. I could see the scar clearly, as clearly as the day it was made.'

'Ah, you remember that,' said Conrad, quietly.

'The funny thing was,' she said, 'I didn't think about the past right away. I thought – Scorpio, and he says he doesn't know his birth sign. But then the memories came rushing back. The door was wide open.'

She paused to gather her thoughts. He whispered, 'Go on. Pretend I don't know. Tell me about it – tell me about *him.* As if I were someone else.'

Charlotte began, while the thunder shook the sky and lightning flickered, 'I was twelve. We were in this villa on Santa Vittoria. On a hill amid olive trees looking down on a bay with silvery sand. There were two more families near-by, with kids, as old as me. We got on like a house on fire.

'They teased me about not swimming but always wanting to be by the water. But in the end they accepted it, the way kids do – that's how I was, so . . .

'That holiday seemed endless. Even the rows I was having with my father seemed to ease off, as though we were both relaxing. My mother was happier.

'Then this family moved into an empty villa. We didn't know at first, but they were foster-parents. The boy wasn't theirs. Maybe if we had known we'd have been . . . kinder to him.'

'You think so,' Conrad suddenly broke in bitterly. 'Kids are worst of all – no limit to how cruel they can be.'

Charlotte took Conrad's hand now. The fingers were long and cool in hers.

'He was older than the rest of us, a couple of years. Tall, thin, awkward, too intelligent, too mature. But we just found him strange. You know how strange kids get treated. In the end we tormented him. He would blush, stammer, get in a rage and storm off. We'd giggle and nudge each other. He should have ignored us. But he always came back for more.'

Charlotte breathed in deeply. The air had become closer, the light dimmed. Soon, she thought, it would be too dark to work, though it was not midday. She squeezed Conrad's fingers.

'I was worst of all. This boy followed me around. He was into astrology, like me. He knew ten times more. When he found me on my own he'd talk about destiny, how we were linked together – Scorpio and Pisces, both water signs, both intense, both different from other people. If I'd been older I might have handled it better. I began to feel threatened.

'He wanted us to do something to prove to the world that we were linked by fate. One day he persuaded me to go to a cave along the beach. He had a plaster on his chin. Then when we were on our own he proposed a ritual that would bind us together. I should have gone away, but I was fascinated, paralysed.

'He tore off the plaster and showed me this raw Scorpio sign carved in his jaw. Then he got out this knife and wanted me to do the same. The sight of that wound made me hysterical. I started to laugh. His eyes were so piercing. I guessed he was wounded, but I could not stop this crazy laughing. If I'd hit him across the face I could not have hurt him more.

'I ran away with him shouting behind me. I ran straight into the sea. The sandbank shelved suddenly and I went down; the water was over my head.

'My father must have been on the beach, heard me and came running. When he pulled me out he was so angry. I know now he was wild with anxiety about his crazy daughter. He thought I was drowning myself. And I could not tell him what had happened.

'That row went on all day. That evening when my father and mother went out for his birthday supper, I should have gone. But I refused . . . He . . . Darren Conway knows what happened.'

'Oh, yes,' said Conrad, 'there is nothing he does not know.'

Charlotte swallowed, then placed Conrad's hand in her lap. The coolness of the fingers penetrated the fabric of her dress to the warmth of her thighs.

'What Darren cannot know is how he reached me that day. What he did, crazy as it was, was hidden inside me until the day I saw that scar again. You do get a second chance, Conrad. Our destinies *are* linked together. You believe you arranged our meeting, but I think there is far more than that.

'Five years ago I was too locked up in myself, too young to respond. That must have hurt you. I was too immature to recognise love, but not now. But you were not. You did not forget. You didn't rest until you found me again.

'Now I can repay my debt to that boy. I can match his feelings, your feelings. Conrad, I've learned one thing from all this, more important than anything else. I love you.'

Chapter Twenty-five

Conrad stood up, loosened his fingers from hers and walked to the window. As he reached it a flicker of lightning made the scar on his face show up white and clear. He turned to face her, voice low.

'You have no idea, Charlotte, what your words mean to me – to that boy in the cave, how much you have repaid him already.'

'Already?' She was baffled by his words, his tone and the hint of a smile on his lips.

'Already. What you have told me is only one very small chapter of the story which I have to tell you. There is so much you do not know, Charlotte.'

'Tell me, Conrad.' She moved towards him but he held up his hand, 'Sit down, Charlotte, and listen. I'll tell you the full story of our lives. In five years they have been so tangled together they can never be separated, unless one of them ends.'

A chill, like a small breeze, touched her. 'Conrad? I don't understand.'

'You will. Now you have told me what your real feelings are, I must tell you about mine. You must know the real meaning of our destinies . . . Charlotte. People think I'm a liar and a cheat.'

'Conrad!' she protested.

'Don't be sentimental. That's what they think. Ask your friend, Matthew. They think I made up my life story to suit myself. Let me tell you, Charlotte. Other people wrote my life story for me, people I never saw, people I do not want to know.'

The smile grew, showing his strong white teeth.

'What I have been doing is rewriting that story, making it come true. And at the same time, I've been rewriting yours as well. There was no other way.'

From his pocket Conrad drew sheets of paper and held them out. 'You know what these are?'

She nodded without speaking.

'I wrote your horoscope. And you wrote back as instructed, and told how closely events fitted the prediction. You thought it was a little experiment in astrology. But it was an experiment with life.

'Your picture, "Doomwater", it's good. You could be really good. But even if that picture was rubbish, I'd still have bought it, though, let me tell you the truth, art does nothing for me.'

Conrad's arm made a circle, his fingers pointing round the room, now deep in shadow, now lit by shafts of lightning in the sky outside.

'All this was just for you, this weekend. I watched you from the moment I found you again. I watched you struggling with your memories, every baffled look when you caught sight of that scar under the beard. I could hardly believe my luck when your clever friend started probing my past, when he found that old press picture. He thought he was separating us but he was drawing us closer together.

'I watched you in the churchyard, reliving Santa Vittoria, though my part in it was still hidden behind that closed door. Then at the chosen moment I showed the scar and you thought you were beginning to understand.' He paused.

'You began that journey back into your own life and at each stage, without knowing it, you wrote down your thoughts, each turn which drew you closer. I brought you here and watched your feelings grow, watched your friend's efforts to warn you, watched you reject him, and choose me. Then came that phone call which took him away from here today.

'When that happened I almost began to believe in fate, in happenings you cannot control.

'You see, Charlotte, you had to break with Matthew, because you believed me, not him.'

A sudden, deafening peal of thunder shook the mill. A flash of lightning showed Conrad's face in clear profile.

'But, Charlotte, Matthew was right and you were wrong.'

Chapter Twenty-six

Charlotte sprang up, the tension inside her unbearable.

'Wrong, Conrad? What does that matter? What if I am wrong – if I love you?'

He spun round to face her. 'Love me? I believe you do. You're made for love. You're Piscean, romantic, vulnerable, you have to have love to shape your life. People love you. That clever friend loves you, he's crazy about you . . .'

'No! Not – now.'

'Yes, now, still. I know the signs. I was crazy about you five years ago, crazy enough to tell you, crazy enough to put it to the test and you . . . you laughed that stupid, screeching, girl's laugh.

'You don't fully understand feelings, Charlotte Dawson, because you've never fully known them, because you don't know the other side of love, and that's hate . . . yes . . . hate.'

His eyes glittered as another lightning flash lit the room.

'Conrad, stop this please. Why are you tormenting me like this?' cried Charlotte.

He circled round her like a great cat round its wounded prey.

'Because I want you, for once in your little life, to know what it's like to feel pain, real pain. Not to imagine you suffer, but to suffer.'

Darting forward, he flipped open the lid of the basket and drew out a knife. Its keen, slender blade flashed. Charlotte screamed and started for the door, but he was there before her, arms held wide.

'No, Charlotte. Five years ago you ran away. Not now.'

He held the knife up in front of her face. She flinched. But he was holding out the handle.

'Let's see, a little test. Do what I did, when I loved you. Carve your birth sign on your chin, like I did. Convince me. Words are easy. Actions, Charlotte, actions.'

'Conrad, stop. You're ill. It's the strain of . . .'

His laughter rose, 'I never felt better than I do now. I've been sick these past five years, you have no idea how sick.

'But I'm cured, now. Shall I tell you what my

cure is, guaranteed for every fool that ever believed they loved someone else?'

Conrad threw down the knife and began to circle round her again, always keeping between her and the door as she swung round, mesmerised, to face him.

'My cure is hate, Charlotte, hate. You think love makes the world go round. It doesn't, it's hate. Hate and greed, the will to take and to destroy, that's the force that rules the lives of all of us.

'Love, Charlotte. No lover on earth could do what I have done, go to the lengths that I did, for you, out of hate.'

Charlotte's head began to spin. Soon she felt all sense would go from her and she would leave this waking nightmare behind. Her reaching hand struck a chair. She sank down into it. Conrad stopped his circling and began to talk quietly, almost to himself.

'I carved Scorpio on my chin. But I have no idea when I was born. I chose Scorpio when I read those two words, "Vengeful, vindictive". I chose my birth sign, as I chose the rest of my life.'

He moved towards her and laid his hand on her

head, gently. All her remaining strength drained away.

'Calm down,' he murmured, 'listen. It will not take long.'

'Please, Conrad,' she whispered. 'I can't take any more. I told you I loved you. You've humiliated me. I deserved it, maybe. Now the scores are even. Isn't that enough? Can't you just let me go?'

He stroked her hair, 'No, Charlotte, not yet. You must follow the story through to the end. You think you know what happened, but there is more; all that you have suffered in the past five years, all that is my work, too.'

She lifted her head, eyes wide, glistening with tears. 'Yes, my suffering. I thought it had come to an end. All these years remembering how my parents died; I thought that meeting you again would help me free myself from that guilt . . .'

'Yes,' he stroked her hair again. 'You feel guilty about their death. You believe in some strange way that you caused it, but you do not understand . . .'

Something made Charlotte twist away, struggle up, knocking the chair over. But he seized her by both arms. Those slender fingers were terribly strong.

Thunder rolled outside, lightning flickered. A silence followed, then he said, 'That death – it was no accident. I killed them, Charlotte . . . and you were to blame.'

Chapter Twenty-seven

Conrad's arms supported her now. Without them Charlotte would have fallen. His voice was caressing.

'It was so stupid, but life's stupid anyway. I meant to kill you. You were the only one to know how I had been humiliated. With you gone, I could wipe that out.

'So I fixed your father's car. Even then I was an expert on hardware, before I realised that software is what counts, the software of the mind. You know, Charlotte, your mind is in my hands now.

'Your parents would have to go too, but I didn't even think of them. I pictured you rolling down that hill, the metal screaming, the fireball . . .'

Charlotte groaned, but Conrad went on.

'I hadn't realised how strong your will could be, how far that quarrel with your father could go. I watched from the villa courtyard, heard your father call to you, "We won't wait for ever". I could not believe that you were escaping me.'

Charlotte's body shook. Conrad mechanically patted her shoulder.

'You heard him, lying up there in your bedroom with the Venetian blinds opening and shutting in the wind. You can still hear him, can't you, Charlotte, just as you did in the bedroom up at the house yesterday.'

'Yes, yes,' murmured Charlotte. Her body began to rock to and fro.

Conrad's mood seemed to change. He chuckled, 'There's a joke, too. He said something else, which you didn't hear, before he gave up on you. He said, "Oh all right, have it your own way. We'll go by the coast road, but come on."

'When I heard that, I realised that my plan hadn't gone wrong. Killing you would have been a mistake. I would have ended the story and I wanted it to go on. Maybe fate knew better than I. You were meant to live on and remember – that was my revenge.'

Charlotte raised her head, eyes blank, voice dull, 'Yes, Conrad. You've had your revenge. I believed in my heart I killed my parents. Now I know for sure. It was their lives for mine, and mine's not worth living.'

Conrad's long, slender fingers touched her cheek, softly.

'You understand. I knew you would. You believe in love. Now you can prove it. Look.'

He pointed to the picture on the wall.

' "Doomwater", your end recorded. Your farewell note. No one who sees it will doubt what it means.'

'Yes.' The words came in a gasp from Charlotte's lips.

Conrad held up the horoscope sheet.

'The moon has turned, Charlotte. Sun, Mercury and Venus have moved into your opposing sign. Pluto, that's for elimination, isn't it, is moving into Scorpio, that's for intensity. Now is the time for you to resolve all guilts and fears that have filled your mind these five years. Time to resolve them in your chosen way.'

Beyond the thunder which boomed with increasing frequency and the lightning flashes which lit the room like the sun, Charlotte heard the rain which deluged from the purple sky.

Her whole being was flooded with water, dark green water, which flowed over her, shutting out harsh light, cruel truths. Now it could all end . . .

Conrad had flung open the door. Through the downpour, the millpool below lay level and calm, dark and inviting under the darker dome of the sky.

'The bridge rail's down, Charlotte. Nothing in your way. I've brought you to this moment. But the last steps you have to take on your own.'

He stood back. No longer conscious of her actions, Charlotte moved across the white room and out into the curtain of the storm.

Chapter Twenty-eight

Charlotte plunged into a world of water. The threatening arch of purple sky was torn apart by giant, branching bolts of lightning. Her head rocked with each massive peal of thunder. Blinded and deafened, beaten by the sluicing rain that streamed over her shoulders, she moved unresistingly towards the depths of the millpool.

She could not see the bridge, but walked on, clothes plastered to her body, mind blank. Soon it would be over, the guilt, the torment; there would be silence, and peace.

From a great distance, as in a dream, she heard someone call her name, and as in a dream she was held back, her way was blocked. Her feet pushed forward, but she no longer moved. Again and again, she heard her name.

Unseen hands were on her arms, pressing her back. As she leaned forward, so this invisible presence forced her back. She resisted, they were stronger.

Confused, she slipped on the rain-drenched grass. She began to fall but was held up, eased back once more.

Slowly the noise of pelting rain died away. Her heel struck against stone, then wood. She was on the threshold of the mill door, then inside the high white room again. Stunned by the storm which echoed round the mill, she looked down.

Water streaming from her body formed a circle on the yellow wooden floor tiles. She shuddered and slowly became aware of herself and others.

To her left was Conrad, face pale with shock, the Scorpio scar gleaming whiter in the half-light of the room. In front of her, shirt and jeans sodden black with rain, face set, eyes fierce with fury and concentration, was Ker.

An idiotic thought played in her mind. These two under her eyes, one so handsome, one so ugly.

Ker guided her backwards to a chair and she sat down, bewildered, weary. Conrad spoke, baffled:

'How did you get here? I thought . . .'

Ker laughed, a short barking laugh.

'I know you did. But there's nothing wrong with my father. I made that up. Two can play that game,

Mr Durrant. I wanted to understand, Charlie, just what hold this crook had over you . . . and now I know.'

'You cunning . . .' Conrad began.

Ker laughed again, 'No one easier to fool than a con artist. Besides, I'm Gemini, aren't I? Two-faced.'

Now Ker spoke to Charlotte again, 'I wanted to see how far he would go. I've got my answer. I heard it all. He set you up, Charlie, preyed on your fears. He wanted you to destroy yourself.'

He swung round to Conrad. 'It hasn't worked, has it? There's no victim, in this scheme.'

'What do you mean?' Conrad's voice was tight, small.

'I mean, I'm taking Charlotte back with me. And you are not going to stop us.'

'I don't think so,' Conrad's voice was stronger now, his eyes on Charlotte, not Ker. 'You coming makes no difference.'

'No difference?' Now Ker was unsure.

'Ask Charlotte.'

Ker looked at her, seeing as if for the first time the look of blank despair framed in her auburn hair, lank and dark with rain.

'No, Ker. It doesn't change anything for me. I

was just ready to put everything right, when you stopped me.' She rose from the chair, firmly as if her mind had focused once more. 'This is my own decision, my own choice. Conrad has not made me do anything. He's just made it all clear, my guilt for everything, for my parents' death . . .'

She took two steps forward. Ker leapt back before the door, 'No, Charlie. You are not going out.'

He turned to Conrad again, voice lower, as if trying to reason with him. 'If Charlotte goes, the world will know you drove her to her death.'

'No, no.' Conrad's voice was just as reasonable. 'No one will know what happens down here, will they?'

Ker's voice cracked, 'I'll tell them.'

Conrad smiled, 'Matthew, for once that analytical brain of yours let you down. No one is here, except Charlotte. You are at home with your sick parent. Everyone saw you go. I'm in my room working. All my staff know that.'

'Oh, yes,' said Ker. 'You fixed that. Tape recordings of your voice on the phone. High tech makes deception so easy. But,' his voice rose on a triumphant note, 'high tech can reveal the truth, can't it?'

Reaching to the belt at his back, Ker slid into view a slim red and black case.

'You ought to appreciate this, Mr Durrant. I borrowed it from the *Sentinel*. Snooper's gear. Picks up conversations at thirty metres. It's all on tape. Anything happens to Charlotte and this is public – all media. You know what that means.'

As Ker held up the machine, Conrad sprang with incredible speed, one hand lashing into Ker's face. As he flinched, Conrad's other hand snatched the recorder. Without halting in his forward movement, he flung open the door, took one step out into the storm and hurled the box from him. The splash as it hit the water of the pool was swallowed up in the noise of the rain.

Feet astride he turned to face them. 'Let's begin again, Matthew. Charlotte is here alone. That painting on the wall is her farewell message – no words, none needed. Now, let things take their course. Don't be selfish. Let Charlotte decide her own destiny.'

Ker's face, softened by despair, turned to Charlotte. But she did not look back. Her eyes were on the door again and the water beyond. She murmured, 'Yes, let me go, let me go.'

Chapter Twenty-nine

Ker moved to block her way. The sudden violent movement broke Charlotte's trance for a second. She looked at Ker, the familiar ugly face, the sad eyes, the wet strands of hair on his forehead.

But he was looking over her shoulder at Conrad, seeing in a split second his expression change to something wilder. With a snake-like sideways lunge, he snatched up the knife then, straightening, shouldered Charlotte aside and brought the point to bear on Ker's face.

In that moment Ker's expression was transformed. His eyes took fire. 'You'd cut my throat to give Charlotte her freedom? So that's it. Murder Number Three?'

The knife point wavered. Ker went on. 'Go ahead, then. Do it. You've got your alibi. Angela will testify in court that you were in your room. She has no choice, poor cow, with her criminal record. You'd blackmail her, just as you tried to blackmail Charlotte.'

Ker placed himself more firmly in the door opening.

'You're hesitating, aren't you, and I'll tell you why. You daren't use that knife. It's all bluff, isn't it? You didn't kill Charlotte's parents, did you?'

Ker turned to face Charlotte, her face blank with amazement.

'I've spoken to your grandmother, Charlie. I've read those inquest reports, talked them over with her. It was a simple accident, a boulder fallen into the road – a tragedy you had no hand in – and neither did this pathetic creature here.'

Ker reached forward and pushed the knife in Conrad's hand to one side. Now he advanced, obliging Conrad to retreat in step with him, talking as they performed this strange dance.

'You rewrote your life because you could not face the truth. You hated your mother for the way she brought you into the world. She needed help and pity and got none. You couldn't even spare her a thought for what she suffered. All you wanted was to make other people suffer.'

Ker circled Conrad. The knife-hand hung down, the eyes enlarged, became blacker, the scar-marked jaw trembled. Ker was merciless.

'You made other people believe your fantasies, conned their money out of them. You fooled them. So far so good. But then you started to believe the lies yourself. Goodbye Darren, hello Conrad. You're not evil, you're sad.'

Ker turned to Charlotte and laughed. 'He's not even a successful speculator. All this place is run on borrowed money. His operation's going down the pan. That's why the little friends have gathered this weekend, for a rescue operation.'

'That's not true!' Conrad's voice was high-pitched.

'Not true? How would you know what's true and what's not? I'll tell you, Mr Durrant. Do you know what the news is today?'

Conrad's eyes stared.

'The Government's crashed in Tokyo. Financial scandal and tomorrow the market goes through the floor, followed by Singapore, Hong Kong.'

Conrad threw down the knife, dragged from his pocket a slim mobile phone. But before he could dial, Ker spoke again.

'Go on, use your mobile. Blow your alibi. Your staff think you're in your room, don't they, dealing with the situation. Go on, tell them the truth. You're down here playing this sick game with Charlotte, while it's all falling to pieces up there on the hill.'

Conrad sank on to the couch, head in hands. Ker taunted him, 'You daren't find out. You've lost touch with the truth, you've lost touch with life. You're finished.'

The savagery of his voice shook Charlotte. 'Don't, Ker, don't destroy him.'

Ker rounded on her, 'What's wrong, Charlotte? Can't you bear the truth? Do you want to stay in dreamland with your guilt and your fantasies about destiny and drowning?'

Conrad stared as the two confronted one another.

'Your gran told me. Years ago, on a picnic here at the mill. You used to swim. You were only five, but you could swim.'

Charlotte stared, but she did not see Ker. She saw and smelt a warm summer day, by the water, heard laughter and shouts.

'You took the little raft your father made and when they weren't watching you paddled out to the middle of the pool, it overturned and you went down, right to the bottom. By the time he pulled you out you'd almost drowned.'

Charlotte felt the dark green water close over her. She swayed, fought for breath. But Ker went on again.

'Not fate, nothing mysterious. Just something to know, to understand. Something to fight against. Truth can hurt, Charlie, but it can't kill. Only lies can do that.'

Ker stopped speaking. Conrad had moved from the couch, eyes alight with some new determination.

'Where are you going, then, Conrad?' Ker demanded. 'Going to put matters right, eh? Make one last effort to put your little fantasy world together again?'

As Conrad came face to face with him, Ker's voice changed as if he had suddenly realised something. He reached out to take hold of Conrad.

'No. Don't. Not that!'

The two collided, Conrad screaming, 'You are not going to get in my way! You are not going to stop me!'

With crazy strength he carried Ker with him through the open doorway. As Charlotte sprang after them, the two, locked, struggling together, crashed over the broken bridge rail and vanished into the rain-lashed depths of the millpool.

Chapter Thirty

For one freezing moment Charlotte stood on the bridge, one hand clenched over the remains of the rail, body swaying over the gap where Conrad's desperate rush had carried him, with Ker in his grasp, into the millrace.

Beneath her the waters foamed and boiled, but beyond, the current swept into the wide surface of the pool, still and black, beckoning her, calling her.

Somewhere below that surface rolled the bodies of two people whose lives were twined with hers as surely as those of her parents had been. Now they were gone and she could feel the inner core of her being drawn out, leaving her wasted and empty. Now there was nothing to keep her from the green depths.

Her knuckles, clenched white on the rail, began to loosen, her body began to bend down. She would fly after them.

Then the spell was broken. Into her vision, in mid-pool, an arm, long and pale, rose above the water.

Life was re-enacting her picture. 'Doomwater'. This was her real moment of destiny. Could she go beyond that truth?

In that moment she heard again Ker's voice, recalling how she had nearly drowned in this pool, boldness carrying her into danger.

Past, present, future came together in her mind with a jolt which shook her free from her hold on the bridge. Now she seemed to see herself as one who paints a picture.

She saw the figure, sodden clothes moulded to her body, turn and run from bridge to bank, from bank down the slope through the trees to the flat shore.

Suddenly she was aware of rain pounding her face, head and arms, reeds catching her bare legs, brambles slashing at her skirt. Pain brought her into herself again. Now she was no spectator, no watcher of events any more.

Power rushed through Charlotte as she loosened her belt, stripped off the clinging skirt and let it fall away. Snatching at her top she dragged it over her head, stumbled, then flung it away with a shout.

Now she was bounding free, taking huge strides, feet smacking into the mud on the margins of the pool. She was at the furthest point, opposite that stretch of water where she had seen the upstretched arm.

Turning, she raced into the pool, leaping and plunging. Now she was half-wading, half-swimming, going in deeper. With heart-stopping suddenness the lake bed gave way beneath her.

The half-light vanished, the rain no longer beat on her. She was falling down. No, not falling. Her arms struck out, propelling her forward. Every trace of fear had gone. Charlotte's eyes opened wide to those green depths, familiar from dreams. This was her world and she was in command.

Ahead a dark shadow, a strange beast, four arms, four legs, twisting, writhing. She lunged at it, grappled, took hold of clothing and hair, and pulled with all her might, kicking her way towards the top again. Her heart thundered, pain shot through her shoulders.

She knew even as she clawed away that she did not have the strength to bring both these locked bodies to the surface before the air in her lungs gave out.

She ran her hands over hair and faces till her probing fingers found a chin, a jawline. She searched for that scar and then, thrusting violently this way and that, she tore the bodies apart.

Taking one in her arms, Charlotte kicked out. Her lungs, muscles, strained and heaved. But above her the green gloom lightened. She drew up her knees and flung her legs down rhythmically, again and again, while her arms held fast the chosen body.

An explosion of light and bubbles round her head, the air screaming into her lungs. Freeing one arm she beat the water, lashing out with both legs, head pointing the way to the shore.

When she feared her strength would last no longer, her toes sank into soft mud. She was half upright, stumbling into the reeds, dragging her burden behind her.

Charlotte laid the figure streaming on the grass and flung herself beside it. Taking hold of arms, swinging them in wide circles and finally throwing herself on top and forcing her lips on to the face beneath.

After another age of torment, a shudder shook them both. Beneath her the eyes opened, staring at her in amazement, then looking past her.

Above, the storm clouds were packing away beyond the tree-lined slope. The sun rose above them and from the dark mass into the clear blue arched a double rainbow.

'It's stopped raining,' said Ker.

'I know,' answered Charlotte, stupid with relief.

His eyes focused on her face. 'I tried to stop him,' he said.

'I know.'

Chapter Thirty-one

The storm died away, but in the weeks that followed, another storm blew up with increasing force. Before the official inquest could take place the media moved in to conduct their own unofficial post mortem.

Spurred on by the fury of Conrad's creditors, left high and dry with the collapse of his operations, journalists began to dig among the debris. And some, at least, of the staff Conrad left behind, were ready to talk.

Conrad's life was a gift, his 'financial empire', his youth, his earlier time in court. 'Billions made and lost at an age when other kids are thinking of dates and A levels,' gasped one tabloid.

Others went one better, dug deeper. Now it was the 'fatal triangle' with the 'tempestuous red-headed artist' and the 'journo-sleuth'.

For two weeks Charlotte's life was a crazy succession of phone calls, interviews, pursuits, sometimes desperate, sometimes absurd. Afterwards she remembered chiefly Gran drenching a bunch of cameramen with the garden hose.

Her ordeal ended only when, in the coroner's court, she relived the events of Conrad Durrant's last day. The coroner treated her with compassion, speaking of the efforts she, and Ker, had made to save Conrad.

'Such a meteoric career as his at so young an age, a career handling billions of pounds in financial interests must, tragically as it has turned out, be vulnerable to quick changes of fortune,' he told the court.

Angela, dressed in black, her face pale, gave evidence calmly. She confirmed that Conrad's dealings had suddenly run into uncontrollable crisis, just three days before his death.

There was a terrible silence in the court and Charlotte's heart felt like ice as the coroner asked Angela, 'There have been suggestions, insinuations I might say, that Conrad Durrant's interest in Charlotte Dawson went beyond an admiration for her artistic work and that this was in some way linked with the circumstances of his death.'

Journalists on the press bench eyed one another and began to take more detailed notes as Angela answered, her voice taking on a sudden warmth.

'No sir, I don't believe that. He admired her painting, which he found by chance. But that was all.'

'No – emotional interests?'

Angela's eyes turned for a split second towards Charlotte across the courtroom, then she went on, 'Conrad and I knew one another for ten years. We were as close as people could be. There was no room for a third person.'

She bowed her head and the coroner kindly told her to sit down.

Returning an open verdict he sternly called on the media to end the speculation on Conrad's death.

Next day his remarks were reported in the more sensational papers, together with pictures of Angela in black, white-faced, leaving the courtroom. There was little mention of Charlotte and soon the story died.

The media lost interest in the rise and fall of Conrad Durrant and turned to another royal divorce, another sex scandal with a Government minister. The circus moved on. Charlotte and Ker could begin to pick up their lives again.

*

One warm autumn afternoon Charlotte and Ker stood in the churchyard and looked down at her parents' grave. Leaves from the trees above drifted down. Ker bent to brush one or two from the headstone.

Maybe we should just let the leaves cover it completely, thought Charlotte. Then she said quietly to herself, 'No, I shall come here every month as I've always done, and be with them again.'

More loudly she said, 'I can face them now, Ker. I can accept they've gone.'

'Yes,' he answered. 'And they'll be happy that you have a life. That is what they wanted.'

Turning, they walked back between the graves. The soft air, with its faint scent of cut grass, gave Charlotte a strange feeling of sadness, yet she knew that underneath she was happy as she had never been before.

Near the gate they stopped by a freshly dug grave. A simple stone resting on the raw earth carried the name of Conrad Durrant and the date of his death, aged nineteen.

Someone had placed a small bunch of flowers in front of the stone.

'Angela,' murmured Charlotte, Ker nodded.

'She tried to warn me about him,' she went on. 'I thought she was jealous. But she knew I was in danger somehow. But she could not tell all that she knew because she loved him.'

'Yes,' said Ker. 'He thought he had a hold over her. He was right. But it wasn't what he thought. She didn't need blackmailing to stay loyal to him. But then he didn't understand loyalty.'

'Couldn't,' said Charlotte.

'Right,' answered Ker, then went on awkwardly, 'let's go, shall we? I'm afraid I find churchyards . . .'

She took his arm. 'I know. Tell you what. We'll go and get a pizza and drive over to Harford Mill. The people running it don't mind if you go down to the pool.'

He looked at her, surprised, 'No kidding. You actually want to go back there?'

'Why not? Might even go swimming.'

'You are truly crazy.'

'Right. I'm Pisces. Only we call it inspired, temperamental, you name it.'

They left the churchyard and walked down the lane to where the little painted car sat by the grass verge. As they took their seats she turned, half joking, half triumphant to Ker and said, 'Well, the prediction worked out, didn't it?'

'Ha,' he retorted. 'There were at least two, maybe three, ways it could have turned out.' Then he spoke more quietly. 'If you'd left it to destiny, Charlie, I wouldn't be here now. When we were in the pool, you couldn't save both. You had to choose.'

'Don't, Ker.' She put a hand on his arm. 'If someone were to find that tape buried in the mud, what would they make of it?'

He shrugged, 'A story, that's what it is, a story.'

Charlotte busied herself with the ignition then said, 'Ker. When you told Conrad he was fantasising, how did you know his story wasn't for real?'

Ker looked out of the car window. 'I didn't, Charlie. I believed him. But I lied to him. I took the risk because there was no other way I could get through to him. I just lied and lied and as it turned out, I was telling the truth.'

'I don't know how you did it,' she said in wonder.

Ker smiled. 'Simple. I'm two-faced. I'm Gemini, aren't I?'

'But you don't believe in astrology, Ker!'

'See what I mean?' he laughed.

Charlotte dropped her hand from the ignition key, then turned, put her arms round Ker's shoulder and kissed him. His arms came awkwardly round her and the kiss went on.

At last they released one another. Charlotte looked at Ker and a silly thought ran through her head.

He hasn't turned into a prince. But I've turned into a frog. Water's my element.